Alfred Elton van Vogt, one of the all-time grand masters of the science fiction genre, was born in Winnipeg in 1912. The son of Dutch parents, he left school at an early age and worked in various clerical and manual jobs while writing in his spare time. Although his first literary successes were achieved outside the SF field, he was a regular reader of speculative fiction and his first story in the genre, *Black Destroyer*, was published in John W. Campbell's *Astounding* in 1939. *Slan** (1946) has been considered the most outstanding of his novels but his consistent inventiveness and variety can be found in his many other novels and short stories. Among his most famous works are: *The World of Null-A* (1948), *The Voyage of the Space Beagle** (1950), *Empire of the Atom* (1957), *The Mind Cage** (1958) *The War Against the Rull** (1959), *The Wizard of Linn* (1962), *Rogue ship** (1965), *The Silkie* (1969), *Quest for the Future* (1970) and *Darkness on Diamondia* (1972). His short story collections include: *Destination: Universe!** (1952), *Away and Beyond** (1952), *The Far-Out Worlds of A. E. van Vogt* (1968) and *The Best of A. E. van Vogt* (1975).

'A. E. van Vogt is one of the enduring primitives of science fantasy. His plots are almost always incredibly complex and surprisingly potent ... If you haven't tried van Vogt yet, you should'—*Edmund Cooper, Sunday Times*

* Already available in Panther Science Fiction

Also by A. E. van Vogt

A. E. Van Vogt

The Undercover Aliens

PANTHER
GRANADA PUBLISHING
London Toronto Sydney New York

Published by Granada Publishing Limited
in Panther Books 1976
Reprinted 1980

ISBN 0 586 04324 1

Copyright © 1950 by A. E. van Vogt
Originally published under the title *The House
That Stood Still*

Granada Publishing Limited
Frogmore, St Albans, Herts AL2 2NF
and
3 Upper James Street, London W1R 4BP
866 United Nations Plaza, New York, NY 10017, USA
117 York Street, Sydney, NSW 2000, Australia
100 Skyway Avenue, Rexdale, Ontario, M9W 3A6, Canada
PO Box 84165, Greenside, 2034 Johannesburg, South Africa
CML Centre, Queen & Wyndham, Auckland 1, New Zealand

Made and printed in Great Britain by
Richard Clay (The Chaucer Press) Ltd
Bungay, Suffolk.
Set in Linotype Pilgrim

Granada ®
Granada Publishing ®

Prologue

His first awareness was of a man saying quietly from the darkness: 'I've heard of such wounds, doctor, but this is the only one I've seen.'

He realized, then, that the bullet which had been fired at him out of an alleyway – he remembered that clearly – must only have wounded him, and he was still alive. Still alive! ... His joy dissolved like jelly in warm water, as he sank again into deep sleep. When perception returned, a woman was saying:

'Tannahill ... Arthur Tannahill of Almirante, California...'

'You're sure?'

'I'm his uncle's secretary. I'd know him anywhere.'

It was the first time he had thought of having a name or place of origin.

He grew stronger. And then, suddenly, there was movement. 'All right,' a voice whispered, 'ease him through the window.'

Darkness, and a feel of being swung out and down, then a swaying movement. A man laughed curtly, and a woman said: 'If the spaceship isn't there on time, I'll —'

He was next conscious of a powerful forward movement, with an intense throbbing sound somewhere in the background. The sensation ended finally in darkness. And then a man's voice said: 'Of course the funeral attendance will be large. It's important that he look dead at the service...'

His body swelled with resistance to the idea of being a pawn in a dream. But the all-enveloping paralysis held him quiet as death, while rich, solemn funeral music played somewhere near. And held him like a vise in the terrible moment when a lid was clamped into place.

The dirt of the grave made a hollow sound as it struck the wooden box inside which was his coffin. Darkness pressed like a blotter over his mind, but something inside him must have continued the desperate fight. Because, suddenly, he had the sharpest awareness of his long sleep.

He was still in the coffin, but a cool draft of fresh air was blowing across his face. In the blackness, Tannahill put out his hand. On all sides and above, he touched cushiony satin, but after a minute the air was wafting as coolly as ever into his nostrils. As he began to strain again in a more conscious horror, he heard movement. Digging sounds.

Somebody was opening his grave.

A man's voice said: 'All right, lift the box, and get the coffin out fast. The ship is waiting.'

The reaction was too great for human endurance. When he awakened the next time, he was in a hospital bed.

I

It was three days before Christmas. And Stephens had stayed late at his office to finish some work that would leave him with a free conscience over the holidays.

Later, he came to regard his presence in the building as the most important coincidence of his life.

He was putting away his law books just before midnight, when the phone rang. He picked up the receiver and said mechanically, 'Allison Stephens.'

'Western Union,' said the girl at the other end. 'Night telegram from Walter Peeley, Los Angeles, for you, sir.'

Peeley was the chief attorney for the Tannahill properties. It was he who had appointed Stephens as local administrator for the estate. Stephens wondered blankly: What now? Aloud he said: 'Read it, please.'

The girl did so, slowly: 'Arthur Tannahill due to arrive, or already arrived, in Almirante, last night or tonight. Hold yourself on call, but please do not push yourself upon him. It might be advisable for you to wait till after Christmas before introducing yourself. Mr. Tannahill has just emerged from a prolonged hospital convalescence, the result of an accidental shooting; and he seemed very secretive. He plans to spend some time in Almirante. His exact words were that he wanted to "find out something". Give him all the assistance he asks for, and be your own judge as to the extent of your relationship with him. He is in his early thirties, your age bracket, which should help. Remember, however, that the Tannahill residence known as the Grand House does not concern you in your capacity as local agent unless Mr. Tannahill makes some direct request of you in connection with it. This is just a word of caution. Good luck.'

The girl finished: 'That's the message. Would you like me to read it again?'

'No, I've got it. Thank you.'

He hung up, locked the drawer of his desk, and turning, paused to gaze out of the great window. Only a few scattered lights were visible, the main part of the city of Almirante being out of sight to his left. The sky was pitch dark, and there was not a glint of water to indicate that the Pacific Ocean was less than a third of a mile distant.

Stephens scarcely noticed. He was disturbed by the wire he had received. The overall tone of the message seemed to suggest that Peeley was concerned and uncertain. On the whole, however, the advice was good. If the Tannahill heir was acting queerly, then his lawyers would have to be careful. It would be foolish, for instance, for him to lose the agency because the young man thought him a nuisance.

'I'll call him tomorrow,' Stephens decided, 'and place my services at his disposal. If that offends him, then I won't be here long anyway.'

He paused in the outer hallway to jiggle the door to make sure it was locked. And he was standing there when, clear and unmistakable, a woman's high-pitched moaning cry came from somewhere in the remote distance of the interior of the building.

Stephens twisted about.

At first there was no sound. But as he relaxed he began to hear the vague noises of the separate units of the building still reacting to the absence of the day-time swarm of human beings, and to the changing temperatures as the cool, damp air from the ocean encroached upon the land. Hardwood floors shifted, crackling faintly. Blinds flapped in open windows. Doors rattled.

There was no further indication of human presence. 'As the agent for this place,' he thought frowning, 'I suppose I should investigate.'

The Palms Building was a spreading structure on a deep lot. The corridor on which his office opened was long, and two dim overhead lights shed a pale radiance on it. The middle corridor had three ceiling lights and the far end corridor two. No one, and nothing out of the ordinary was visible along any of the three.

Swiftly, Stephens walked to the elevator and pressed the *UP* button. The response was immediate. The elevator door slammed. The electric hum of the motor and the whine of the cables expanded upward. And stopped. The door rolled open. Jenkins, the night operator, said cheerfully:

' 'Lo, Mr. Stephens. Getting home kind of late, aren't you?'

Stephens said, 'Bill, who else is up here?'

'Why, uh, only those Indian worshippers upstairs in 322. They —' He broke off, 'What's the matter, sir?'

Stephens explained grudgingly. He was already chagrined at his excitement. A single phrase of Jenkins brought the disillusionment. Indian Worshippers! He remembered 322 dimly from the rent books of the building. It was occupied by a Mexican firm.

'Well, they're not exactly Indians,' Jenkins answered his question. 'They're white enough except for two of 'em. But Madge says the place is full of Indian stone images.'

Stephens nodded in rueful understanding. Part of the Tannahill fortune derived from early Mexican sculpture, and after becoming agent for the estate, he had read up on it. An unpleasant subject. Barren, barbarous, wretched people – that was his reaction. But the scream was explained. It became a simple product of one of the innumerable cults whose members moaned and groaned and cried and shrieked in every sizable town along the west coast.

'I think,' said Stephens, 'we'd better knock and —'

The second scream, muffled, drawn-out, terrifying in its suggestion of unendurable anguish, cut him off. When it had finished, Jenkins' face was a grayish hue.

'I'll get the police,' he said hastily.

The elevator door slammed, and the cage fell creaking into its abyss. Stephens was alone again, but this time he knew where to go.

He went with the reluctance of a man who had no desire to get mixed up in something that might interfere with the pleasant routine of his life.

The sign on the door said: MEXICAN IMPORT COMPANY. A light glowed dully through the frosted glass panel, and Stephens could see shadows inside. They were human shadows, for they moved slightly. The sight of so many made him cautious. Very gently, he tried the door knob. The door, as he had expected, was locked.

Inside the room, a man began to speak in a low, angry voice. The words varied in distinctness, but enough came through for Stephens to follow the meaning.

'... There is no such thing as separate action ... You are with us, or against us ... The group acts nationally and internationally as a ...' There was a murmur of agreement that drowned out the rest of the sentence; then: 'Make up your mind!'

A woman's strained voice said: 'We've got to stay even if there is an atomic war, and you'll have to kill me before—'

There was a snapping sound, and she screamed with pain.

A man uttered an earthy curse, but Stephens didn't hear the words that followed. He pounded on the glass with his fist.

Inside the room, the confusion ended. A shadow detached itself from the group and came toward the door. The lock clicked, and then the door opened. A small, yellow-faced man with an enormous nose peered up at Allison Stephens.

'You're late,' he began.

A startled look flashed into his face. He tried to shut the door, but Stephens moved his leg and his palm forward and, using the power of his hundred and ninety pounds, pressed the door open against the other's desperate resistance. A moment later, he stepped across the threshold, and said loudly:

'I'm the manager of this building. What's going on here?'

The question was rhetorical. What was going on was quite apparent. Nine men and four women were standing or sitting in various tensed positions. One of the women, an amazingly good-looking blonde, had been stripped to the waist; her ankles and wrists were tied with thin ropes to the chair in which she sat sideways. There were bloody welts on her tanned back, and a whip lay on the floor.

From the corner of one eye, Stephens saw that the little man with the big nose was drawing a spindly object out of his pocket. Stephens didn't wait to identify it. He took a step, and with the back of his hand struck the other's wrist. The weapon, if it were one, glittered with a crystalline brightness as it spun through the air. It hit the floor with a curiously musical sound, and slid under the desk out of sight.

The little man uttered a curse. His hand moved and, from somewhere on his body, he drew a knife. Before he could use it, another man nearby said sharply:

'Tezla, stop it!' He added resonantly to the others: 'Release her! Let her get dressed!'

Stephens, who had drawn back from the knife more amazed than alarmed, said: 'You can't get away! The police are coming.'

The man gave him a thoughtful look. He said in an unhurried, speculative tone: 'So you're the manager of the building ... Allison Stephens ... Captain in the Marines, appointed two years ago, law degree from UCLA ... Well, it seems harmless enough. What I'd like to know is how did you happen to be here at this hour?'

He turned away as if he didn't expect an answer. Neither he nor the others paid Stephens any further attention. The man and two women who had been untying the prisoner finished doing so. Four men stood in a corner beside several stone images, and talked in low tones. Tezla – the only one who had been named – was down on his knees getting the spindly object from under the desk where it had fallen.

The tableau held a few seconds longer. Then somebody said: 'Let's go.'

They began to stream past Stephens who, feeling himself outnumbered, made no effort to stop them. 'The back stairs,' a man's voice said quietly from the hallway. In a minute, there was no one in the room but Stephens and a very white-faced young woman who was struggling to get into a blouse. She succeeded, and grabbed for a fur coat that lay on the floor behind a desk. She swayed as she picked it up.

'Careful,' said Stephens.

She was sliding into the coat now. She turned. Her eyes narrowed. 'Mind your own business!' she said shortly.

She started toward the door and then, as the clang of the elevator came from the corridor beyond, she stopped and turned back. She mustered a smile.

'I ought to thank you,' she said somberly, but no friendliness showed in her green eyes.

Stephens, who was beginning to relax again – though he was startled by her ungrateful remark – said satirically, 'Your decision to thank me couldn't, I suppose, have anything to do with the arrival of the police.'

Footsteps were near in the hall now. A police patrolman loomed in the doorway. Jenkins hovered behind him, and it was he who spoke: 'You all right, Mr. Stephens?'

'What's been going on here?' said the officer.

Stephens turned to look at the young woman. 'Perhaps the lady can explain it.'

She shook her head. 'I don't know why you were called, officer. Somebody has made a mistake.'

Stephens blinked. He was astounded. 'A mistake!' he said loudly.

She studied him. Her eyes were green pools of innocence. 'I don't know what you *think* happened, but we were having a little ceremonial here, and suddenly' – she turned to the officers – 'this gentleman was pounding at the door' – she indicated Stephens.

'Ceremonial!' said the officer, looking around the room and taking in the stone figures with what seemed to Stephens to be an expression of comprehension on his face. Stephens could imagine what the other was thinking, and he could hardly blame the man. His own surprise at the denial was yielding to a disgusted desire to get the thing over with. Nevertheless, he explained that he 'thought' he had heard her being whipped.

The patrolman turned to the girl. 'What do you say to that, madam?'

'It's all a mistake. It was a ceremonial only.' She shrugged, and admitted with apparent reluctance. 'I suppose there were some grounds for Mr. Stephens believing what he did.'

It was evident to Stephens that the incident was just about over. The officer did ask him if he wanted to lay a charge, but that was merely a formality. Without the victim's corroborative evidence, there was no point in taking action. The girl ended the affair by saying:

'May I go now, officer?'

She didn't wait for an answer, but slipped past him into the hallway. The click of her heels receded into the distance.

Jenkins stirred. 'I'd better get back to the elevator.'

The policeman did not linger long. Left alone, Stephens surveyed the room, and wondered what actually had been going on. What he had heard, now that he thought it over, didn't make much sense. The stone images of whatever ancient gods they were supposed to be stared at him with their stone eyes. The silence crept in around him.

He remembered suddenly that the small man who had answered the door had expected someone else, someone so near in size to Allison Stephens that he had momentarily made a mistake in identity. Chilled, Stephens took a hasty look along the corridor. But there was no one.

He re-entered the office, and he had his finger on the light-switch beside the door when he saw the woman's purse lying near the desk, where her coat had been. Without hesitation he walked over and picked it up. He fingered it dubiously, then opened it. He found the identifying card he wanted. *Mistra Lanett*, he read.

Once more, he looked around the drab outer room of the Mexican Import Company. And one thought kept recurring to him. What kind of national and international policy would have made a group of cultists whip one of their members because of an atomic war?

Frowning, Stephens carried the purse down to his own office and then took the elevator to the street floor.

'Goin' to the Tannahill place?' Jenkins asked.

Stephens came out of his reverie, and his first thought was that Jenkins had heard about young Tannahill coming home. He said at last, cautiously, 'Why should I go up there?'

'You ain't heard?'

'Heard what?'

'Murder.'

Stephens' mind jumped to the thought that the Tannahill heir had been killed. 'Oh, my God!' he said, but before he could ask, Jenkins went on:

'The police found the Negro caretaker lying in one of those old wells at the back of the house.'

'Oh!' Stephens was momentarily relieved, then he frowned as he remembered the import of the message from Peeley. He glanced at his watch. Half past twelve. Hardly the time to introduce himself to the Tannahill heir.

Outside, he walked to the corner from which many times he had glanced up at the Grand House. It took several seconds before the vague outlines of the house showed up against the night sky above the darker bulk of the mountain on which it stood. There was no light that he could see. Satisfied that the place was deserted, Stephens went to his car and drove home.

Inside the house, on the way to his bedroom he paused to knock on the door of the housekeeper, intending to tell her that he wanted an early breakfast. The door was ajar and he remembered he had given the woman a two weeks' vacation to visit her family. She had left the day before.

Stephens undressed, put on his pajamas and dressing-gown, and he was brushing his teeth when the front door bell rang three times, swiftly. As Stephens headed toward the front hall, a key fumbled in the lock. The door swung open and Mistra Lanett slipped in. She was breathing hard. She banged the door shut, and slammed home the bolt. She faced Stephens.

'I couldn't wait,' she gasped. 'They're after me. Turn out the lights, bolt the back door, and the patio doors, and phone the police.'

He must have been too slow for her. Because she brushed past him, and he heard her in the kitchen. The sound of the bolt clicking came very clear and distinct. And it was that which startled Stephens into action. He bolted the patio door of his bedroom and of the adjoining den. He met the young woman coming out of the second bedroom. She whisked past him and began to turn out lights. In less than a minute, with his help, they were in darkness. And still she was one mental jump ahead of him. In the blackness he could hear her slowly dialing a number. There was silence.

'There's no answer.' Her voice was strained. 'And the line seems to be dead. They've cut it.'

A prolonged pause. Finally, very softly:

'I wonder if you would mind attending me. I've got a needle beam burn in my side and – and it's hurting me.'

2

In the intense darkness of the living room, Allison Stephens groped his way to the chesterfield. Needle beam! he was thinking, vaguely. What could that mean? 'Where are you?' he asked.

'I'm lying down.' The answer was low-toned.

Stephens knelt on the floor beside her. The strain of the moment was on him. The blackness made the affair nightmarish. He had a mind-picture of men outside on the verge of breaking in.

Abruptly, that changed him. He had been feeling the reluctance again, the unwillingness to be mixed up in something that was not his business. All in a flash, his horror yielded to a blinding, furious anger.

He remembered his Nambu. He jumped to his feet and raced into his bedroom. The Luger-like grip of the Japanese souvenir braced him. It was the seven bullet variety, a very effective automatic pistol. He hurried back to the living room and knelt beside Mistra Lanett again.

He felt the change inside him now, the alertness, the willingness to commit himself; the grim determination to see the incident through.

'Where were you hit?'

'My side.'

It was a whisper, the information not very helpful in that darkness. The fact that she could talk at all made him feel better. He recalled how she had raced around the house. Fear must have stimulated her, of course. Perhaps her present weakness was only reaction.

'Think I could carry you to the housekeeper's room?' he asked. 'Her window overlooks a ravine. They'd need a ladder to climb up to it. We could turn the light on.'

He didn't wait for her answer. He fumbled over her body in the darkness, hesitated as he touched her bare thigh – her dress must have pulled up – then swiftly slid one hand under her knees, the other around her shoulder.

'Hang on,' he said encouragingly.

She weighed less than he had thought. He put her down on the bed, and clicked on the light. As he turned from the switch, he saw a thin trail of blood running from the door to the bed. She looked very pale as Stephens started to un-button her blouse. She was wearing a mink coat over a gray suit, with a white blouse under the jacket. The lower end of the blouse was soaked with blood. It had already stained her skirt and there was a red, sticky streak on the lining of her fur coat.

Stephens decided against removing the outer clothing, since it would require her to sit up. He unbuttoned the jacket and the blouse; and then fumbled his way to the kitchen for a knife. With its sharp point he penetrated the blank wall that was her slip. Underneath was the wound.

It took a minute to get hot water, and several minutes to wash away the covering of blood. The bullet had evidently passed through the flesh just under the surface. Strangely, both the entrance and the exit, which were about four inches apart, were cauterized as if by heat, and the wound was bleeding thinly from within. Examining it, Stephens doubted if she had lost much more than a few tablespoon-fuls.

He couldn't feel alarmed about it. He had seen men almost literally floating in their own blood without dying. And this was nothing. He saw that the young woman was bending forward, peering at the damaged flesh. Her face took on an expression of annoyance. Then she lay back.

'I'll be damned!' she said in disgust. 'It's practically a miss. To think that I was scared stiff.'

Stephens said, 'I'll get a bandage.'

He used several layers of surgical gauze held in place by adhesive tape. He worked with a sense of urgency, holding his breath for long intervals so that it wouldn't interfere with his hearing. But when at last he stepped back to survey his handiwork, there was still not a sound from the night outside. Stephens looked down at the woman tensely.

'What's the matter?' he said. 'Why aren't they doing anything?'

She was lying back on the pillow. She studied him, a faint frown creasing her cheeks. 'I'm twice in your debt now,' she said.

Stephens was not interested in debts. 'What do you think they'll do?' he asked.

This time she considered his question. She said finally :

'It all depends on who else is out there besides Cahunja.' She smiled grimly. 'I know Cahunja is among them because he's the only one who would work himself into a mood to fire at me. But where his own skin is concerned he's extremely cautious. However, if Tezlacodanal is with him they won't give up once they have started. They're all afraid of Tezla, who is one of the damnedest little vipers that ever lived.'

She smiled up at him, with mock sweetness. 'Does that answer your question?'

Stephens scarcely heard. His mind was on the danger, not the words that described it. It seemed to him that, if there had been more than one or two, surely they would by this time have tried to enter the house. He thought about that for a moment, with narrowed eyes; and then he went out into the hall.

'I'll be right back,' he called over his shoulder.

He headed for the front door, and stood peering through the glass into the darkness. The sky was still clouded; the night silent. He could see nothing and no one. He made the rounds of the inside of the house, examining the catches on the windows, and testing the bolts on the doors. Everything was in place. Partially relieved, he returned to the housekeeper's room.

The young woman opened her eyes and smiled at him wearily. 'I'm sleepy,' she said.

He spent the rest of the night in the lounge. It seemed to offer the best position from which to defend the house. He dozed and sat up, alternately. Not once, while it was dark, was there a threatening sound. About dawn, he fell into a deep sleep.

Stephens woke to the realization that it was broad daylight. He glanced at his watch; it showed five after one. He sat up with a sigh, and then tiptoed along the hall to his own bedroom. As he passed the housekeeper's room, he noticed the door was closed. He had left it slightly ajar.

It stopped him short. He knocked. No answer. He knocked again, then tried the knob. The door was unlocked, and the room was empty.

He stood there for a moment, annoyed at the realization that he felt rather let-down. It was almost as if he had enjoyed the episode, and yet, as he remembered it, he had been tense and grim all the time, even in the moments when he was putting on his best show of being relaxed.

Perhaps it was the woman. Once, in San Francisco, he had had a casual affair with a girl as beautiful as Mistra Lanett. That was a long way back now. Still, these days he looked for more in a woman than good looks. It was hard to imagine himself falling for a stranger.

He guessed then that he pitied her. She was so obviously in a state of distraction. Hunted, she herself had sought refuge with a stranger. And yet, there seemed little doubt of her courage. Even as she was being whipped, with no apparent hope of rescue, she had talked back to her captors.

Frowning, Stephens unlocked the front door, and went outside. The sun was shining, and he could hear the sea a few hundred yards away. The bungalow was a Tannahill property, set back from the coast highway. It was isolated from other nearby residences by a series of low hills; it had a heated swimming pool, a three-car garage, and four bedrooms, each with private bath. He had rented the place to himself for sixty-five dollars a month.

For a time he had felt guilty about that, even though it was Peeley's suggestion. Gradually, however, he had come to regard it as part and parcel of the pleasant existence that he had enjoyed ever since becoming the Tannahill agent.

He walked now along the driveway till he saw the tire tracks, where a car had backed off the pavement, and turned around. It gave him satisfaction to be able to guess from the placing of front and rear wheel markings that the car had been a big one, possibly a Cadillac or a Lincoln.

He returned to the front of the house, and peered up at the telephone wires, where they came in from the highway. Presently, he traced them down the side of the house.

They had been cut just above ground level. He'd have to call the phone company as soon as he got downtown, and report the vandalism. He would have liked to phone Tannahill, but that also would have to wait.

He slipped out of his dressing-gown and pajamas, and took a running dive into the pool which was just outside the living room patio door. The water was chilly, and he headed hurriedly back to the steps. He was climbing out when he saw the face staring up at him from the depths.

Just for an instant the shock was terrific. For that one moment he thought it was a body. And then he reached down into the green blur of water – and had the mask.

It was thin and sticky, and threatened to come apart in his fingers. He drew it gingerly out of the water, and laid it on the concrete. It seemed to be made of a very thin, filmy substance, but that was not what amazed him.

The thing had recognizable features. They were slightly blurred at the edges, where the water had damaged them. But there was no doubt who they looked like.

It was the *face* of the man who had prevented Tezla from knifing him.

Stephens left the mask on the concrete, dressed, and, shortly before two, started for his office. For some time he had been remembering that Mistra's purse was there. He hadn't really examined it thoroughly the night before, and it was possible her address was in it.

It was time for some explanations. He'd have to try again to get in touch with Tannahill, but, entirely apart from that, the problem of the 'Indian worshippers' who talked of atomic war, whipped their own members, and used weapons without mercy, had to be forced out into the open.

First, Mistra. As a hunted member of the group, she was a key to the mystery.

Fifteen minutes later he had the contents of her purse spread out on his desk. A cigarette case, a change purse, a billfold, keys, a cardcase, an expensive handkerchief, and a small cloth folder. He examined them in that order, becoming progressively more disappointed. None of the articles was even initialed.

He was unwrapping the cloth folder when a thought struck him. No lipstick or powder, no make-up of any kind. The reason seemed obvious when he finished opening the cloth folder. Inside was a mask of a woman's face. It looked surprisingly natural, but unlike anyone he had ever known. Stephens stared at it, and felt the color drain from his cheeks. He thought weakly: What the hell is going on here?

He calmed, and examined the mask. It was semi-transparent, and extremely thin.

Stephens groaned. The trouble was he didn't know enough to decide what this meant and what he ought to do. It was too soon to draw any final conclusions. He needed more information, and he needed it quickly. Events were forcing the issue. There was still the fact of the torture and attempted murder of Mistra —

The shocking reality of that directed his next action. For some minutes he had been increasingly aware that elsewhere in this very building was another possible source of information. Now, without hesitation, he went out of his own deserted office and along the corridor to the Mexican Import Company.

The door was locked. He let himself in with his pass key and pulled up the shades. Everything looked unchanged. The stone figures proved to be clay on closer examination, which meant that they were probably hollow. He lifted one as a test. It was heavier than he expected. He was about to replace it when he saw that an electric cord ran from under it.

The cord was plugged into a floor socket.

Stephens felt quite blank. He was only mildly curious. He disconnected the cord, and eased the figure over on its side.

The wire disappeared into a tiny hole in the clay. It was impossible to see what was inside, or what might be the purpose of the electrical connection. He replaced the figure, leaving it just about as he had found it – and turned his attention to the desk.

The drawers were locked. But one of the keys he had taken from Mistra's purse unlocked them. Inside were bills, invoice forms, account books, a file of letters that began with some variation of: 'Dear Sir: We are shipping you art objects to the value of —', another file of letters on copy paper which were mostly acknowledgments of receipt of the shipments, or 'Herewith find our check', and, finally, a third file in which were cartage forms on which were printed the addresses of individuals to whom the 'art objects' had been sold. Most of the letterheads had Mexican date-lines.

Stephens counted the name 'Waldorf Arms' twenty-seven times before he admitted to himself that he had his clue. He had seen the place several times. It was a five story apartment building in a good district, rather oddly constructed, as he recalled it, and from all accounts very exclusive.

It was annoying that none of the forms contained a name, but at least he could write down some of the addresses given, and check later to see who lived at them.

He wrote down an even dozen.

Back in his own office, he remembered Tannahill, and phoned the Grand House. His call was answered almost immediately by a gruff voice: 'Who's speakin'?'

Stephens gave his name, startled by the roughness of the other's tone. Could this be the Tannahill heir? The man at the other end said:

'Oh, the lawer! Tannahill ain't here, Mr. Stephens. I'm

the police guard, Sergeant Gray – the only one around here except for the electricians, and they just come. You heard about the murder, huh?'

'Yes.'

'Well, Mr. Tannahill's gone down to the courthouse to talk to Mr. Howland about it.'

Stephens suppressed an exclamation. He had a sharp conviction that Tannahill would not appreciate having to do things like that on his own. Hastily, he thanked the officer, and broke the connection.

A few minutes later, he was on his way to the district attorney's office.

3

As Stephens entered the deserted foyer of the courthouse, he heard the first faint sounds of merriment from somewhere in the building. It was not until he had vainly rung the elevator buzzer several times that the truth dawned on him. The Christmas party was in full swing.

He climbed the stairway; and peered into the open doorway of Howland's outer office. His initial impression was of utter confusion. Men and women were sitting on the edges of desks, and even on the floor, or standing around in groups. Scores of bottles were in view, and liquor glasses were everywhere.

No individual seemed to be aloof from the group, so if Tannahill was among them, then he had joined the party.

He found Frank Howland sitting on the floor behind a desk in the far corner of the room. Stephens poured himself a drink, and waited while the district attorney grew aware of him and peered up blearily over a glass of brown liquid.

Recognition came only after several seconds. Howland let out a piercing cry : 'Hi, Stephens!'

He scrambled to his feet and flung one arm around Stephens' neck. He was a tall man, about as big as Stephens, who was on the strapping side himself. Before Stephens could brace himself, he was flung around by the other's powerful grip, to face the room.

'Fellows and gals,' Howland bellowed, 'I want you to meet my old pal, Allison Stephens. Did this guy ever strike it rich – and I still don't know how he did it. He's agent for the estate that owns the whole damn country around here.'

He waved his hand with the glass in it to take in a generous half of the world. The glass banged against

Stephens' shoulder, and the liquor in it slopped down as far as his trousers. Howland didn't seem to notice, but Stephens cursed him silently for a fool. The district attorney was roaring in a deep baritone voice:

'I want everybody to understand that Stephens is my pal … I'm inviting him to this party, so treat him just like you would me … Okay, Stephens, I want to talk to you later on, but right now the place is yours …'

With a grin, he shoved Stephens into a milling group of women. 'He's yours, gals, and still single.'

They were good-natured about it. One of them took out a handkerchief, and dabbed at his coat, murmuring, 'That ham actor – he used to be an actor, you know.'

Stephens drank for a while with a small group of females of widely varying ages. When he finally broke away from them, he had no idea what the conversation had been about. He found Howland entwined with a tall, stately girl who laid herself limply down on the floor the moment Stephens pulled the district attorney's arms from around her waist.

'Go away!' she mumbled. 'I wanna sleep.'

She seemed to sleep immediately. The big man appeared unaware for a moment that he had been detached from his girl friend. It seemed to dawn on him suddenly, for he squirmed in Stephens' grasp.

'What the hell are you trying to do?' he said loudly. 'That dame has been like an icicle ever since I took office, and just when I get myself wrapped around her, you —'

He stopped. He blinked at Stephens, seemed to sober somewhat, and grabbed his wrist.

'Just the man I want to see,' he said. 'Got something I want you to read. Meant to show it to Tannahill, but he didn't turn up. Came special delivery this morning.' He smirked knowingly. 'Pretty smart guy, that boss of yours, but I'd give a dollar to know what his game is. Come in to my office.'

He unlocked a drawer and took out a folded sheet. Stephens unfolded it and read frowningly. The letter was typed, but it was not signed. It said:

Dear Mr. Howland:

If you will open the grave of Newton Tannahill, you will find that the coffin is empty. The resemblance between the uncle and nephew is rather startling, don't you think? Draw your own conclusions about that and about the Negro caretaker who was found dead last night.

With pursed lips, Stephens re-read the note, trying to fit it into the confused pattern of recent events. Whether or not it was true, somebody was evidently attempting to stir up trouble. From the large room outside a dozen throats burst simultaneously into drunken laughter. Somebody shouted something. Glasses clinked with a musical chiming. The babble of conversation continued.

Stephens licked his lips and glanced at Howland. The man's chin was sunk low on his chest and he seemed to be asleep. Howland made a sudden move, and muttered: 'I can't understand it. What would make a man pretend to die so that he could inherit his own money? Doesn't make sense. How could he suddenly look younger?'

He subsided. Stephens shook his head and shoved the note into the drawer from which Howland had taken it. Then he locked the drawer and put the key in the D.A.'s vest pocket. Howland did not stir.

The shouting of the drunks followed Stephens down the staircase. It did not fade out until he had closed behind him the outer door of the building.

He climbed into his car, and sat soberly considering his next move. 'I've got to see Tannahill,' he told himself.

He started the motor, and drove along to a newsstand. In the paper he bought, the account of the death had been cut down to a single column three inches long. It related succinctly how the body of the Negro caretaker, John Ford, had been discovered the night before in a half-filled Mayan 'drowning well' by the newly arrived Arthur Tannahill. All the rest of the front page was devoted to the arrival of Tannahill in Almirante. There was a picture of a slim

young man with a lean, handsome face. It was a tired looking face, but the paper explained that also. Young Tannahill
had for nearly two years been a patient in an eastern
hospital suffering from a serious wound in the head, the
result of an accidental shooting, and he was still recuperat-
ing.

The story gushed over into the inside pages, and became
a sketchy history of the Tannahill family. Stephens, who
had read a somewhat fuller and equally eulogistic account
at the Almirante public library finally folded the paper, and
wondered, what next?

He decided to phone the Grand House again. Sergeant
Gray answered, 'Nope, not back yet.'

Stephens had dinner in a combination restaurant and
cocktail lounge called CONTENTMENT BAR. He felt dissatisfied
with his position. He wasn't doing enough. The worst of it
was, Tannahill must be unaware of the danger he was in.
Nor was Stephens sure of what it was.

He finished the meal, and drank an extra cup of coffee
while he re-read, carefully this time, the news account
about Tannahill.

One of the points made was that '... Young Mr. Tannahill is not known to his fellow townsmen, having visited
here only on two occasions when he was a boy. He went to
school in New York and in Europe. The bullet that injured
him affected him so severely that he remained unconscious
for a year and seventeen days. This does not include the
period from April 24th to May 5th of this year when,
apparently suffering from shock, he wandered from the
hospital. His recovery has been slow, and unfortunately his
memory of certain events of his life remains hazy as a
result of his wound.'

The dates given for Tannahill's disappearance startled
Stephens. 'I can check that,' he thought, *now!*'

With a sense of urgency and excitement he hurried to
the door and outside. It was dark, and that pleased him; for
his purpose needed the cover of night. The knowledge of his
destination gave him an empty feeling, but he had to quiet

the suspicion which had been planted in his mind. As the Tannahill lawyer on the scene, he had to obtain all the information he could. He made the drive to the graveyard at the northwestern part of the city in four minutes, and found a map of the cemetery on the wall of the gatehouse. Having located the Tannahill plot on it, he parked his car under a tree and headed along a dark pathway. When he came to the north fence, he turned east and knew that he was close. He began to peer at the markings on headstones. Five minutes later, he found the Tannahill plot.

He edged along an iron fence and through a gate with an overhead trellis. The name hung down in metal letters from the trellis and even in the dark, lighted by the flashlight from his car, it made a pretty picture. Inside were nearly a dozen headstones. Stephen bent over the nearest. The lettering on it was Spanish, and the name was curiously spelled. It said:

Francisco de Tanequila Y Merida
febrero 4, 1709–julio 3, 1770

The next name was still in the Spanish form. The dates were 1740–1803. The third headstone had the name in an English variation for the first time. Tannehill, with an e instead of an a. That particular forefather had died in 1852. He must have witnessed the beginning of the gold-rush.

Stephens was moving along in a quieter fashion now, the feeling of urgency gone from him. The age of the graves impressed him, the long back history of the Tannahills brought a kind of pride that he was now connected with the family. He tried to picture Francisco de Tanequila being borne down the mountain and buried here on a bright day of 1770. Before the revolution, he thought. Long and long ago. The roots of the Tannahill family were deep in this soil.

He grew conscious of how cool the night had become. A wind was blowing from the sea. It rustled through the trees, and the leaves shook in their steady whispering song, the same song they had sung during all the nights since those quiet graves had been dug.

He bent low, and peered down at the headstone of the end grave. The light silhouetted the name:

Newton Tannahill

Stephens re-read the death date below the name to make sure, then slowly straightened. He felt the weariness of a man who has come to the end of a long trail. Newton Tannahill, the uncle, had been buried on May 3rd, last. From April 24th to May 5th, Arthur Tannahill, the nephew, had been missing from his bed in the hospital.

Stephens was turning away from the headstone when there was a faint sound behind him. Something hard and blunt jabbed into the small of his back, and a voice said softly:

'Careful, don't move!'

Stephens hesitated, and then, realizing that he had no reasonable alternative, accepted the defeat.

4

There was silence in the darkness under the trees of the graveyard. Stephens tensed to take advantage of the slightest opportunity. If they tried to bind him, he'd fight. Behind him, the soft voice said:

'I want you to sit down, cross-legged. Nothing will happen to you if you do as I say.'

It was the use of the first person singular that calmed Stephens. He had been intent on the thought that there were several men against him. But the 'I' had a tone behind it – he couldn't have described it – that left no doubt. This was one man. He had no intention of obeying blindly, however.

'What do you want?'

'I want to talk to you.'

'Why not talk like this?'

There was a curt laugh. 'Because you might make a sudden move. Sitting cross-legged, you'd have a hard time attacking me.' The man's voice lost its softness. 'Get down!' he said sharply.

'What do you want to talk about?'

'Get down!'

The other's tone was hard and convincing, and the blunt object pressed more firmly into Stephens' back. Reluctantly, cursing under his breath, he crouched down. He sat there, still tensed, determined that he would submit to no further indignities.

'What the hell do you want?' he said harshly.

'What's your name?' The voice was soft again. When Stephens had given it, the man was silent for several seconds, then: 'I seem to have heard that name somewhere before. What do you do for a living?'

Stephens told him.

'A lawyer, eh? I think I've placed you now. Peeley mentioned you. I didn't pay any particular attention.'

'Peeley!' said Stephens. The realization flashed on him then. 'My God,' he said. 'You're Tannahill!'

'I'm Tannahill.'

The identification took a tremendous weight from Stephens' nervous system. He rose to his feet, saying urgently:

'Mr. Tannahill, I've been looking all over for you.'

'Don't turn!'

Stephens stopped with his heel dug deeply into the dirt. He was astounded by the sharp hostility of the command. Tannahill went on quietly:

'Mr. Stephens, I don't accept anyone at his face value. So you will just remain with your back to me until we have cleared up a few points.'

'I'm sure,' said Stephens, 'I can convince you that I am the local agent of your estate, and that I am acting in your interests.' He was beginning to realize what Peeley had meant in his telegram. The Tannahill heir must be carefully handled.

'We'll see,' was the noncommittal reply. 'You say you've been looking all over for me?'

'Yes.'

'So you came here?'

Stephens could see suddenly what Tannahill was getting at. He had a brief, vivid picture of himself peering at the names on gravestones with the aid of a flashlight. His mind leaped beyond that to the reason for the presence of the other man. He realized instantly that, before he could ask any questions, he would have to explain his whole position.

As succinctly as possible he described everything that had happened since he had left his house that afternoon. When he came to the note which Howland had shown him, he paused to remark:

'I had thought about that, and it brought me here to check up on a couple of dates.'

The other man made no comment, but waited till Stephens finished his account. And even then he was silent for at least a minute before he finally said, 'Let's sit under those trees. I've got to talk to somebody.'

Stephens noticed that he limped badly. There seemed to be no pain involved, for he settled down onto the grass easily enough. As Stephens seated himself, Tannahill spoke again:

'Do you think they'll open the grave?'

Stephens was startled. He hadn't actually got that far, but he recognized that the question struck to the heart of the problem. He wondered if this meant the grave *was* empty ... He hesitated, thinking of the fact that District Attorney Frank Howland had been dismissed as local agent of the Tannahill estate, and that, being a principal figure in the Adams–Howland–Porter machine, he was in a position to do great damage to his former employer.

He said slowly, 'I'm afraid, sir, I can't answer that question. I've called Peeley, and as soon as he arrives we'll go and see Howland and ask him if he has managed to trace the writer of that note. Have you any idea who it could be?'

'I'll ask the questions,' was the curt answer.

Stephens bit his lip, then said, 'I'll be happy to answer all your questions, Mr. Tannahill, but I do know the local situation, and it's possible I could get at the root of this matter very quickly.'

Tannahill said, 'Stephens, my side of this affair is very simple. I have been in a hospital for a long time, paralyzed in my left side. I was unconscious for over a year after I was wounded. Late last April, I disappeared from the hospital, and I was found on the steps on May 5th, still unconscious. I regained consciousness about a week later. Three weeks after that I received a letter from a woman signing herself Mistra Lanett – What's the matter?'

Stephens had uttered an exclamation. But all he said was, 'Go on, sir.'

Tannahill hesitated, and then continued: 'Miss Lanett identified herself as the secretary of Newton Tannahill, who had apparently died and been buried coincidentally with my absence from the hospital. She went on to say that I would shortly be notified that I was the sole heir to his estate. I was subsequently advised that I had inherited one of the large fortunes of California. I could have moved here then, and hired a hospital staff of my own, but I had two reasons for staying on where I was. The first reason was that I had great faith in one of the doctors at the hospital. He refused all my bribes to get him out here, but he did justify my faith; for I can walk, slowly to be sure – but walk. The other reason has to do with a vague dream-like memory of something that happened to me during the period that I was missing from the hospital. I won't tell you anything about that, but it decided me that, when I came here, it wouldn't be as an invalid.'

He drew a deep breath. 'Events seem to have justified that also.'

He was silent for a long moment, then in a tone that was slightly harsher, he went on: 'On the morning after I arrived here – when I was still at the hotel – I was visited by three men, one of them a small Mexican Indian with an enormous nose. They pretended to be old friends of mine and identified themselves as Tezlacodanal – that was the Indian; Cahunja, who looked like a half-breed, and a chap whose name I can't recall, though it was given. They persisted in addressing me as Newton Tannahill, which, as you know, was my uncle's name. I had no fear of them, but in order to gain time for private investigations of my own, I signed a letter which they presented to me.'

'Letter?' Stephens echoed.

'It was addressed to Peeley,' Tannahill went on, 'and in it I authorized him to continue the payments he had been making to members of the Pan-American Club – that was the name. I added the clause that this authorization must be reaffirmed by me every six months. They offered no objection, and in view of my ignorance of the matter I feel that I got off rather easily.'

'You felt that your life was being threatened?'

'N-no! It was the strangeness of their identification of me as my uncle that decided me.'

Stephens looped his mind back over what Tannahill had said about the letter. 'The phrase "continue payments already made" was definitely in it?' he asked finally.

'Yes.'

'Well' – it was relieving to be able to say it – 'that seems to indicate there was previous association. We can ask Mr. Peeley about it.' He added, 'But why would they think you were your uncle? He was at least twenty years older ...'

Tannahill did not answer immediately. When he finally spoke again, his voice sounded far away, and there was no indication of anger in it. He said:

'Stephens, I am subject to nightmares. In the hospital, I had strange dreams in which fantastic figures appeared. Once I seemed to be in a coffin. Another time I saw myself here in Almirante, California, looking down at the old sea. I remembered the house blurrily, as if I was gazing at it through a thick haze. Of course, Peeley had sent me some books about it – there are several, you know – and what I read probably colored my dreams. According to the books the Grand House is old beyond the memory of white men. As you may know, its architecture is pre-Mayan. When you see the long formal steps that run the full length of the front, you get more an impression of a temple than of a house, though the inside has been very skilfully made over for living purposes. When I was in the coffin —'

He stopped. In the darkness of the cemetery there was silence. Finally: 'If you read the papers,' said Tannahill, 'you know the rest.'

Stephens said, 'A little while ago you mentioned Mistra Lanett. Did you say she was your uncle's secretary?'

'Yes.'

Stephens pondered that in a gathering astonishment. It was one thing he'd never have suspected. The connection of the Mexican Import Company and *that* ruthless group with Tannahill was something he'd have to think over. It would be dangerous to drag it in now when the other was still suspicious of him. The whole thing sounded as fantastic as Tannahill's own story. Stephens thought grimly: We could never tell anything like that to an Adams–Howland–Porter courtroom.

The realization that he was already thinking in terms of a courtroom galvanized him.

'Mr. Tannahill,' he said earnestly, 'we've got to get to the bottom of this affair as quickly as possible. I have an awful suspicion that somebody is trying to pin a murder rap on you. The murder of the caretaker. That's putting it bluntly, and whether it turns out to be true or not we've got to be prepared for it. Several times in your story you referred to a memory of having been buried alive. I'm not sure you noticed that you did so; it came in rather incidentally. Just what did you mean?'

There was silence.

'Mr. Tannahill, I honestly don't think you should keep anything back right now.'

Silence.

Stephens yielded. 'Perhaps,' he said quietly, 'you would prefer to wait until Mr. Peeley arrives and we can talk over with him everything that has happened.'

This time Tannahill spoke. His tone was far away, as if his mind had retreated into a great distance.

'It was a dream,' he said. 'I dreamed I was buried alive. I told you I was subject to nightmares.'

His voice changed. 'And now, Mr. Stephens' – more briskly – 'I think we had better conclude our interview. I have several plans in mind, and I will outline them to you tomorrow if you will come up to the Grand House to see me. Perhaps by then you will have succeeded in contacting Peeley. Tell him to come down here at once.'

He stood up slowly, and leaned on his cane. 'I think, Mr. Stephens,' he said, 'we had better leave here separately. It wouldn't do if Mr. Howland discovered that we had come' – he hesitated, then finished quietly – 'that the Tannahill heir and his lawyer had come into a graveyard to check on the date of a man's funeral.'

Stephens said, 'There are several bad aspects to it. I hope you have a license to carry a gun, sir. That would —'

'I don't carry a gun.'

'But —'

There was a chuckle in the darkness, and then the shadowy cane came up and jabbed Stephens just above his belt.

'How does it feel?' said Tannahill.

Stephens said, 'Oh!'

'I may call tomorrow, but perhaps not till after Christmas,' Tannahill went on, 'and we'll arrange a meeting. Now, is there anything else?'

'Yes.'

Stephens hesitated. He had a question so vital to the whole issue that he felt he might be rushing things to ask it now. And yet, either now or later, it must be answered. He said slowly:

'The papers mentioned that your wound had seriously interfered with your memory. And your story gave that an even greater importance. Are you willing to tell me the extent of your amnesia?'

The reply came after the barest pause. 'I remember nothing of my life before I woke up in the hospital. I can talk, I can think, I can reason, but my memory for anything before I woke up last spring is virtually a blank. I didn't even know my own name until I heard it while I was partially unconscious.' He laughed curtly. 'I assure you it has made things difficult. And now, Mr. Stephens —'

He paused, then continued earnestly, 'I hope you realize that I have trusted you with information which I have told no other living soul. I did it because I accept your good faith, for the moment at least, and because I need other people to help me work out this situation.'

Stephens said, 'You can count on me in every way.'

'You'll tell no one, unless I give permission?'

'No one.'

Stephens returned to his car and sat in it for several minutes, considering his next move. He was tired, but he was also anxious about his job. There were just too many fantastic questions without answers. Why was someone hinting that a nephew and uncle were the same man? And why did everyone – including himself – seriously consider this possibility instead of laughing at it? The fact that no one had ever seen the nephew until the uncle was dead was not enough. What was the meaning of the masks – masks so perfectly made that he was willing to accept that they could be worn without being detected? For a minute, Stephens had a complete feeling of unreality, of being involved in a madman's nightmare. He shrugged it off.

The one clue that had emerged sharply from his conversation with Tannahill was the reference to Mistra Lanett.

It seemed to tie in the gang.

Stephens started the motor and drove toward the Waldorf Arms. He had no definite plan, no idea of what he would do when he got there. But he felt stubbornly convinced that it must be a center from which the group was operating, or the name wouldn't have come up so often on the books of the Mexican Import Company.

He parked his car near the building, but did not get out immediately. In the darkness, the unusual domed architecture of the superstructure was only vaguely apparent. Lower down, it was quite an ordinary building, even a little old-fashioned, in its square, brick appearance.

Stephens was about to climb out of the car, when he saw a small man walking rapidly toward the entrance. Unmistakable small man with unmistakable nose – Tezlacodanal, who had drawn a knife on him the night before. Tense with excitement, Stephens climbed to the pavement.

He had unquestionably found a hot trail.

5

From the shadows beside his car, Stephens watched the little man turn into the bright entranceway, and go inside. Swiftly, Stephens followed. He arrived at the door breathless, and took a look through the glass.

Hastily, he drew back, then edged forward again until he could just see the interior. The Indian was standing at a magazine stand. His back was only partially toward Stephens, and he was reading a thin newspaper which, at that near distance, Stephens saw was titled the *Almirante Herald*. He saw, also, that what interested the other was the article about the arrival of Tannahill.

With a shrug, Tezlacodanal tucked the paper under his arm, and started across the spacious lobby in the general direction of the elevator. He nodded to the elevator man, but walked past the elevator and along a brightly gleaming hallway. He paused at a doorway about halfway down, took out a key, fumbled for a moment with the lock, and disappeared. He did not reappear.

Stephens forced his way through a thin hedge and moved slowly along the side of the building. He paused beside a window from which a vague light gleamed through closed venetian blinds.

The window was open, and the blinds moved gently in a quiet breeze that blew slantwise against them. That was the only sound. Nor was there a movement of a shadow against the light to indicate that anyone was inside.

After a determined half hour of waiting for the light to go out, Stephens began to wonder if he had estimated his distance accurately. Was this the apartment that Tezlacodanal had entered?

He made his way rearward, pausing at each window. The blinds were partly open and so he was able to verify that the rooms within were all part of the same suite as the first.

Stephens drew back into the shadow of an overhanging shrub, and once more waited. Time passed slowly, and it grew steadily cooler. The moon came up over the trees to his left, a lemon-colored slice of light that crept higher and higher in the sky. He began to feel the eeriness of his vigil. As a lawyer, he was earning his money the hard way. Only the light behind the blind remained unchanged, a dim brightness, defying his purpose. He grew restless; then he grew angry at Tezlacodanal for not going to bed; then angry at himself for believing that the continuance of the glow meant that the man was necessarily still awake. It was that thought that brought him to action.

He approached the open window and, pressing aside the blind, peered into the room. He saw a divan, a reddish rug, a chair and an open door. It was through this door that the light streamed. It came from a floor lamp standing beside a desk. There were bookshelves visible just beyond the desk and the lamp and several clay figures.

Stephens moved cautiously to the other side of the window. He pushed that end of the blind aside carefully and peered in. Shadows. More chairs. And only reflected light. The open door was not visible. There was still no sign of a human being, nor a sound of life.

Caution was strong upon him now, but he did not hesitate. It took only a moment to push the window high enough for his body. He balanced himself on the sill, took hold of the blind and, lifting it, slid under it onto the chesterfield beneath. He lowered the blind into place, listened for several seconds, then stepped noiselessly onto the rug. Five quick strides, and he was across the room and standing beside the door.

There was no one in the second room, but a partly closed door led from it. And it was as he stood beside it, listening, that he heard from inside the regular breathing of a man asleep.

Stephens did not move immediately. What did he want? Information. But what kind of information did he expect to obtain?

He glanced indecisively around the room. The den was not so large as it had appeared from the window, and all the books were in the one case. Stephens peered at them briefly, and he was about to turn away, intent on his main problem, when his gaze lighted on a title: TANEQUILA THE BOLD. It was a thin volume, and it required scarcely any time at all to slip it into his pocket. Intent now, he skimmed the other titles. They were mostly in Spanish, a language of which he had little knowledge. But there were three others of those in English that interested him. Carefully holding the books he retreated into the living room and to the window.

Safe outside, he grew more and more astonished, not that he had retreated, but that he had ever gone in.

Arrived home, he found that his telephone had been repaired, and promptly contacted the phone company. But his call to Peeley had not yet been put through.

That done, determined to wait up for a reply, he put on his pajamas and dressing-gown and sat down on the living room couch with the books he had stolen. They were all about the Grand House or its family, and he couldn't recall ever having seen any of them before, not even in the Almirante public library's special Tannahill section.

Stephens picked up first the *History of the Grand House*, and glanced at the flyleaf.

Limited First Edition
Fifty-three Copies Published
Privately Distributed
January Eighteen Seventy

He turned the page to the beginning of Chapter One. The first paragraph read:

For a thousand years or more, a remarkable house has stood on a high hill overlooking the old sea. There is no satisfactory record of who built it.

Stephens flicked his gaze down the rest of the page, then he leafed slowly through the next few pages, reading an occasional paragraph and absorbing the gist of the rest. The manner of writing was very positive. It reminded him of historical novels he had read. The author's imagination had pumped up details of what was undoubtedly one of the least known eras in the history of the world: Old Mexico and southern California from A.D. 900 to the coming of the Spaniards.

The intricacy of detail rang false to Stephens. He had enough familiarity with Mayan and Toltec history to recognize that the known details depended upon excavation and deciphering of a crude system of recording facts. Here were the names of priests, of private soldiers, of a man named Uxulax who had been transfixed with arrows for a crime not named. Nearly a thousand years before, this wretch emerged from oblivion, was executed and buried on 'the east side of the hill in a grove of pine trees later chopped down by the Toltecs' – all in two sentences and for no apparent purpose.

The Toltecs, when they came, 'in long lines of soldiery, sweating wearily along the coast in the heat of early fall,' at first intended to destroy the Grand House. But, like the other expeditions that came laboriously up to this remote frontier from time to time, they lacked the equipment to dismantle a marble structure.

The priest-soldiers made an additional discovery. The comforts left by the previous tenants 'who had retreated hastily to the safety of a Pueblo village farther to the north' were superior to anything they had ever had. They salved their consciences by erecting a wooden temple on an artificial mound (so that it towered above the house) and then, Kukulcan apparently satisfied, they used the house as a residence for themselves and their women. The favorite lady of a long line of priest-commanders was —'

The name was blacked out. Stephens stared at the elision, puzzled. There seemed no reason for it, but the ink was extremely dark. Not a trace of the lettering underneath was visible.

Stephens shrugged, and read on. The account now that he was further into it had a fascination of its own. The quantity of the detail built up a picture and a mood. The crisis of the Toltec occupation came when year after year passed without the arrival of a relief expedition. The priest in charge had finally been more than ten years in his office, and, since he was a stupid individual, it was decided by — (another blackout) that he must be assassinated before he discovered 'the secret of the Grand House'.

Stephens' gaze flicked to the top of the next page. And stopped. The first sentence there had no relation to what had gone before. He scowled at the page, and then he saw what was wrong. Pages 11 and 12, containing the details of the assassination, and presumably containing also an account of the mysterious 'secret' of the Grand House, had been torn out.

He put down the history finally, and picked up the Tannahill biography. The title, *Tanequila the Bold*, had its own exciting attraction. The beginning chapters started too soon in the man's life for Stephens. They dealt extensively with Capitán Tanequila's early life, his birth in Northern Spain, his voyages down the coast of Africa, his questionable methods of becoming wealthy and his final voyage to America which ended in the wreck of his flagship, the *Almirante*, on the California shore during a severe storm in the year 1643, more than three hundred years before.

Stephens pondered sleepily on the time, striving to remember the life and death dates of the Tanequila buried in the cemetery. That Tanequila had died in 1770, if he recalled correctly. His impression that he was the first of the line was wrong, evidently, by more than a hundred years.

He turned over the page. The new chapter that began at that point was titled *After the Storm*. So far, Stephens had only glanced idly at the book. That chapter he read from beginning to end.

After the Storm

By noon, we were all ashore, all the survivors, that is. Of Espanta, de Courgil, Margineau, and Kerati there was no sign, and we had no doubt that they were drowned. I regretted Margineau. He was a sardonic scoundrel, but the other three were merely sullen dock scum, who will rot in hell for the trouble they have caused me. To satisfy the crew I will probably have to say a litany for their souls, but for the moment I set up a cross in the sand, mumbled a few words, and then set them to work.

There was actually no time to waste. Alonzo had seen several natives hovering about and we could not be sure that they were the usual stupid, friendly breed. It was imperative that we rescue our weapons from the sinking Almirante.

By two o'clock, Cahunja observed that the storm was abating, and so I sent him with twelve men in two boats to begin the work of unloading and dismantling. The wind and the waves abated hour by hour, and by evening a calm sea was running. By evening, too, we had two one-pounders and a quantity of muskets ashore, so I ceased to worry about the natives, and, in fact, the following morning, I sent out a patrol to make overtures to any that would expose themselves, for the purpose of obtaining food.

It was a wild coast on which we found ourselves. In every direction were low hills, heavy with verdure, for it was winter and there had been much rain. There were several inland marshes near our camp. The thick growth in them swarmed with wild birds, whose squawks and cries never ended all the day. Our food parties shot three deer and located a number of edible roots, which, together with food from the ship, rendered us safe from immediate star-

vation. At no time after the first day were we in danger of
going hungry. In my whole life I had never seen land that
was so abundantly rich and at the same time was favored
with such an equable climate. This opinion, formed during
those first weeks, time has borne out. Here is one of the
most satisfactory year-around gardenlands of earth.

On the fifth day, the sentries brought an Indian into the
camp, a small, ugly man, who spoke excellent Spanish. He
was obviously a scoundrel, and my impulse was to listen to
what he had to say, and then drown him. But he proved too
invaluable as an interpreter, and besides he brought good
news. He informed us of what we had already suspected,
that there was a Pueblo village farther north, and the great
chief who lived in a house on the high hill above the village
wanted us to be his guests, although he unfortunately
would have to be away for some time, and therefore could
not welcome us in person. This information was eagerly received by the women, who had been having a wretched
time of it in the open, but I confess I was suspicious. Why
would any man smart enough to become a chieftain invite
a group of Spaniards to take over his home, when he must
know that it meant his tenancy was at an end on the day we
arrived?

Not that it mattered. With our guns we could defeat any
treachery. Besides, it finally seemed obvious that the so-
called great chief was withdrawing from his home until he
could evaluate the menace we presented. I determined to
kill him the moment he decided that he could safely risk a
return. Such cleverness in a native promised to be dangerous to the new owner, myself, if it was allowed to be successful.

The occupation proved even simpler than anticipated.
We had eight cannon, and by locating these behind stone
embankments around the crest of the hill, we dominated
the countryside. In a week we were in such fine possession
that only heavily-armed Europeans could have threatened
our position. There was no resistance. The retainers of the
mysteriously absent 'great chief' accepted our arrival in the

most normal fashion, and not one of them seemed to think it strange that I should occupy the former owner's bedroom.

As the weeks went by, it grew clear to me that we were due for a long residence. Knowing the captains of my other two ships, and remembering our arrangements in the matter of sharing profits, I did not doubt but that they had carefully neglected to search for me, if they had escaped destruction. It was almost certain therefore that they would by now be on the way to Cape Horn and Spain, and that years might pass before another ship came to this particular stretch of coastline. On this assumption I decided to normalize the position of the crew in the village below.

I went down personally, and had the villagers drawn up before me in long lines, men and women and young girls. It was a fairly simple matter to select thirty of the better-looking women, and then isolate their husbands for immediate execution and burial. From among the widows (and a few single girls) the crew members each selected a woman, and I married them then and there by the Bible and assigned huts on the basis of previous ownership. I understand that for a while there was a problem with the bastards the women had borne the native men, but that was a matter I left for each husband to solve for himself. Within a month life in the village was back to normal.

During the year that followed, my main problem was the development of the land. To achieve maximum results I decided against the enslavement of local people, but determined instead to send out patrols to take prisoners from remote villages. These captives were then instructed in their duties by the natives of the newly-named village of Almirante, who acted in the role of overseers. They never seemed to notice that the work which they extracted from their prisoners was nearly all for my benefit, and not their own. There were unfortunate incidents, but the land under tillage by the end of the year was a tribute to the new system.

At the end of the second year there was still no sign of the former owner of the house, and I concluded that he had correctly appraised the entire situation and that in fact his purpose in surrendering the house had been designed to insure that we did not destroy it. We found no evidence of the Toltec temples which legend said had once towered around the house. They had evidently been torn down, and all vestiges of their presence laboriously removed. It seemed to me, however, that the house itself was an example of Mayan architecture. The palenque style, both inside and out, was very marked, though slightly different from anything I had ever seen in Central America.

These problems did not actually concern me at this time. And they departed even more from my thoughts in the third year when the assassination attempts began. What saved us was my prompt recognition that what happened was not a series of isolated events but the initial moves of the former owner to rid his house of interlopers. The knife that Tezlacodanal stuck into my back could have killed me if he had had the strength to overpower me afterwards. The arrow that struck Cahunja missed his right lung by a hairbreadth. Alonzo was the unlucky one. His mistress, an Indian woman named Gico Aine, successfully stabbed him to death. No attempt was made on the lives of the women, which was an indication of what was intended for them.

Gico and Tezlacodanal (the Indian who had first come to our camp) escaped together. Two other Indians also left, but we caught one of them and executed him on suspicion of complicity, though we had no evidence. This was the first of many attempts at murder, all of which I will describe in detail in a later chapter, since they constituted an integral part of the route that led to our eventual discovery of the secret of the Grand House. This secret which —

The page was torn in half at that point. It had been ripped crosswise, and then down the inside margin. Stephens looked to see if the torn section had been put elsewhere in the book. But all he discovered was that there were seven other pages which had been mutilated. A quick glance at the subject matter leading up to the torn sections showed that in every case the reference was to the 'secret' of the Grand House.

Stephens searched for other references. Finding none, he returned his attention to the chapter he had read, in which the name Tezlacodanal had been mentioned. It was interesting to know that there were descendants. He was still thinking about that, or so it seemed to him, when he woke with a start.

6

A faint dawn light permeated the room. It was so dim that he was just able to make out two human shapes standing beside him. He stared into the dark with the sick tenseness of a man surprised in the night by dangerous intruders. In that first instant, he had no sense of recognition.

A man's voice said, 'Don't move, Stephens!'

The tone held Stephens rigid. There was infinite threat in it. Stephens swallowed and, now that his eyes were growing accustomed to the light, he saw that at least a dozen people were in the room.

Curiously, that relieved him. He realized that he had expected two individuals to murder him out of hand. He didn't expect that from many. There was no clear reason for such a conviction. His mind jumped to it, and that was all.

He relaxed, and thought: This is the group that whipped Mistra!

The two men who had stood over him retreated to nearby chairs. The one who had spoken before, said, 'Stephens, make no sudden moves! We're wearing night-vision glasses. We can see you plainly.'

There was a pause, then: 'Stephens, who are you?'

Stephens, who had been trying to imagine what night-vision glasses were, said involuntarily. 'Who am I? How do you mean?'

He had intended to go on, but he stopped. The unusualness of the question struck into him. The empty feeling came back. The 'gang' wouldn't have asked such a question. They knew who he was.

His thought reached that point; and he said, 'Who are

you?'

A woman sighed out of the darkness: 'I could almost see his mind working. I think he's innocent.'

The man who seemed to be the spokesman for the group ignored the interruption. He said, 'Stephens, at the moment we're not satisfied with your position in this affair. If you really are who you appear to be, then I would advise you most earnestly to answer our questions. If you're not, then of course you will try to deceive us.'

Stephens listened with sober attentiveness. There were implications here of – he couldn't decide. He felt the return of unreality. It struck him that, as Tannahill's lawyer, he might gain a great deal of information. He said almost briskly, 'I don't know what you're getting at, but go ahead.'

In the background, there was a low laugh from the woman who had previously interrupted: 'He thinks he's going to learn something.'

The spokesman sounded irritated. 'My dear, we appreciate your ability to read minds, but please restrain yourself from making these unnecessary comments.'

'Now, he's naïvely alarmed,' said the woman. She broke off tolerantly, 'All right, I'll shut up.'

There was silence, but for Stephens it was weighted now. A mind reader! His instinct was to be cynical; and yet, he sensed depths within depths. Money was involved, and intelligence, and brutality that could whip other humans, and shoot without hesitation.

It tensed him again, and he had an amazing picture of his own position at this moment. 'Why, I'm on trial here,' he thought.

And he didn't know what the charge was.

Before he could speak, the man said: 'Stephens, we've been investigating your back history. And there seems to be no doubt that there was a baby named Allison Stephens born 31 years ago in Northern California. A boy of that name went to public school in a small town, to high school in San Francisco, and, according to the records, Allison Stephens joined the Marines in 1942.'

The speaker paused; and Stephens, whose mind had leaped briefly to a part of the reality behind each description – a mental picture of the town where he had spent his childhood, an incident from high school, the day he embarked for active service – nodded, and waited. These things were accepted realities. The silence grew long; and he had time to realize that they were giving the mind reader a chance to examine his reactions. It staggered him a little; it raised the level of the interview – once again he couldn't decide.

All in a flash his mind jumped to a thought he hadn't had before. He said aloud, amazed: 'Just a minute. Who do you think I am?'

It was the woman who answered: 'I honestly don't believe we need carry this any further. I could see that notion coming, and it had behind it all the emotional surprise that came out in his voice.'

A second man said, 'But why did he sneak into Tezla's apartment?'

'Stephens, answer that to our satisfaction, and you're in the clear!' It was the first speaker.

Stephens parted his lips to describe how he had seen Tezla outside the Waldorf Arms; and then he stopped. He heard the woman say:

'He's angry now. It's suddenly dawned on him that we've had an almighty nerve coming in here and questioning him as if our position was legally sound.'

There was general laughter. When it faded, the spokesman said in an inexorable tone: 'But still, what made him go in? Stephens, don't let your annoyance overcome your common sense. Answer!'

Stephens hesitated. He was impressed by the other's earnestness; and, besides, why not? If one answer would rid him of these dangerous people, he'd better give it. He said quietly:

'I had just talked to Tannahill, and he mentioned Mistra Lanett having been his uncle's secretary. That tied her in with you; and so when I saw' – he hesitated – 'what's his name —'

The woman cut him off. 'I sense a little more motivation than that. I have the feeling that he hoped to locate Mistra. I think he's infatuated.'

They were standing up. A man said in a low tone: 'Get the books he took!'

The door opened. There was considerable shuffling of feet, and presently the sound of several cars starting up. The motor throb faded into the distance.

Stephens examined the door. First Mistra had unlocked it, now these people. It was time to change the lock, though the problem of just how they had all had keys was worth further inquiry. He retired to one of the bedrooms, and for the first time let himself think that the mind reader had missed an important point.

She had failed to realize that he had found the clue to Tezla's residence in the desk of the Mexican Import Company. It seemed rather a vital failure on her part, and left him in possession of several other addresses, which he could now investigate first thing tomorrow morning. Perhaps Mistra was at one of them.

The prospect excited him, and he went to sleep thinking. 'She's beautiful, she's beautiful ... beautiful ...'

Shortly after nine the following morning, he drew up a block from the top address on his list. The number he wanted turned out to be a small estate, the house set well back from the road behind a high iron fence. A small boy, who was passing, said, 'Oh, that's the home of Judge Adams.'

Stephens thought almost blankly, 'But that's ridiculous. Judge Adams wouldn't do —'

He couldn't decide what Judge Adams would or wouldn't do.

It took until eleven o'clock to investigate the dozen addresses he had written down. They were, without exception, among the most important people in town: Judge William Adams, Judge Alden Porter, John Carewell and Martin Grant, owners of the two daily newspapers, the heads of three building concerns, Madeleine Mallory, who owned the only private bank in Almirante, two well-known society women, and a prominent importer. Last, but not least, was J. Aswell Dordee, owner of a large eastern steel works; he was reputed, though still a comparatively young man, to have retired to Almirante for his health.

The list was so imposing that, as it mounted, Stephens began to have the conviction that he had hold of a hornet's nest. His early feeling that he might threaten to expose the members if they continued to go after Tannahill yielded to the uneasy realization that the city was firmly controlled. He drove to the larger of the two newspapers and spent more than an hour in its library, poring over photographs of prominent Almiranteans. He did not ask for specific pictures, and so he found only seven of the people he had identified.

He examined the faces, trying to decide if they could possibly – with the aid of masks – transform themselves into the gang members he had seen. He wasn't sure. He'd have to see them in person, and hear their voices. Even then it wouldn't be final. A voice, so an actor had once assured Stephens, was easy to imitate. As for appearance, without a face to compare also, one person looked much like another of his own general build.

Stephens left the newspaper building, uncertain as to what his next move should be. It was December 24th, a bad day for an investigation. The stores would remain open till 9 P.M., but most office buildings were already deserted. He was anxious to begin a search for the fingerprints of Newton Tannahill, though just how that might be done without the help of the police was a problem. Right after the holiday he would put Miss Chainer to work looking up documents that the older Tannahill had signed. Fingerprints casually left on a paper would not be easily accepted as belonging to any one individual. And yet, it was one of the steps that had to be taken.

Reluctantly, Stephens headed for home; at the last moment, he decided to go by way of the Waldorf Arms.

Having made the fateful decision, it seemed natural to park fifty or sixty yards from the entrance in the hope that somebody would come along. He had been there about ten minutes when the door of his car was opened abruptly and Mistra Lanett, breathing hard, settled into the seat beside him.

'I want you to help me get into my apartment,' she said. 'I don't dare try to run the gauntlet alone.'

7

Stephens did not answer immediately, nor did he move. There was a queer, mixed thought at the back of his mind, half anger, half pleasure. He realized that he was glad to see her, and at the same time he was annoyed that she chose these melodramatic methods of coming upon him. He had to admit that in the past she hadn't had much choice.

He found his voice. 'How's your side?' he asked as matter-of-factly as he could manage.

Mistra made an impatient gesture. 'Oh, that. That healed overnight.'

She had on a green suit that matched the color of her eyes. The effect was startling; it gave a kind of glow to her appearance.

He refrained from saying so. He said slowly, 'I suppose you realize you have a lot of explaining to do.'

He saw that she was looking intently at the entrance of the apartment building. Without glancing at him, she said, 'We can talk when we get inside. Please – let's not waste any time.'

Stephens said, 'You mean – somebody might try to prevent you from going inside to your own apartment?'

'Not if I have a man with me.'

Mistra started to climb out of the car. 'Let's go!' she said.

No one tried to stop them. Stephens, who had been too pre-occupied the previous night to be observant, had time and opportunity to be amazed by what he saw. The ceilings were high and intricately wrought. Rugs obviously worth thousands of dollars lay on the floor.

The elevator stopped at the third floor, and they walked

along a wide corridor under hidden lights that cast a cool, bluish brightness on the ceilings and the walls. Mistra paused before a door of limpidly transparent plate glass. Stephens could see another door beyond it, which seemed to be made of metal and was opaque. Her key slotted into an almost invisible lock of the outer door. It opened with a wheezing sound.

She went inside, Stephens following. She paused in the alcove until the first door had shut behind them, then unlocked the inner door. It opened onto a corridor, the ceiling of which was unusually high – fifteen feet, Stephens estimated.

The room into which she led him was like that also. Stephens saw that Mistra had tossed her stole and purse into a chair, and that she was heading for what looked like a built-in bar.

Stephens took out his Nambu. 'I think I'd better search the place.'

'It's not necessary.' Mistra spoke without turning. 'We're safe here.'

Her assurance did not satisfy him. He headed quickly along a corridor that led to two bedrooms, each with private bath. There was a stairway at the end of the hall with a closed door at the top. The door was locked, but it shocked him mildly to discover that it was metal and seemed very solid.

He returned to the living room, and followed a second corridor to what at first glance looked like a music chamber. Behind glass cases, from wall to ceiling, were record albums.

But that was only the wall facing the door. To his right was what seemed to be built-in electronic equipment. Stephens guessed: record-player, television, radio, and also – he saw after a moment – broadcasting paraphernalia including transformers and control panel. He shook his head, turned, and saw that the left wall was lined with bookcases.

There were many books, but he had a profound curiosity

about Mistra's reading tastes. The first shelves he examined were not very satisfactory from that point of view. They were technical scientific volumes – hundreds of them, he discovered.

He was moving swiftly now, and he came to several shelves of history, about half of them in Spanish. A few English titles he noted were: *History of Spanish Civilization in America, Popul Vuh, Spanish Influences in Old Mexico, The Beginnings of Almirante, Tanequila the Bold, History of the Grand House...*

A tinkle of glasses from the direction of the living room reminded him that a beautiful woman was more important than any book. He found her behind the bar, pouring a dark brown liquid into two glasses. She shoved one towards him.

'Try this,' she said. 'You've probably never tasted it before.'

Stephens sat down on a stool and examined the drink cautiously. It looked like badly discolored water.

'What is it?'

'Try it.'

It was as if he had put a lighted match to his mouth. The fire ran down his throat, and he could feel it burning in his esophagus. He set the glass down, gasping. He felt as if his head were smoking. Tears started from his eyes.

He sat there, ashamed of himself. Allison Stephens, who had gulped his share of liquor, nearly knocked out by one drink. He blinked the wetness from his eyes, and saw that the girl was sipping her drink, and watching him with amusement.

'Don't give up,' she said, encouragingly. 'The taste is like classical music. It wears better.' She smiled. 'Better than any other liquor, I mean.'

Stephens took another drink. The fiery effect was still there, undiminished. But this time he did not choke or cry. When it was down, he looked at the young woman.

'I repeat,' he said, 'what is it?'

'Octli.'

Stephens must have looked blank.

'An old Mayan drink,' Mistra explained. 'This, of course, is a special version of my own.'

The reference to Mayan took Stephens' mind back to the books she had in her library. He took another drink, felt blurred again, and then said slowly, 'What's all this about? Who are these people who were whipping you?'

'Oh —' She shrugged. 'Members of a club.'

'What kind of club?'

'The most exclusive club in the world,' she said, and laughed softly.

'What are the requirements?' Stephens was persistent, though he already had the feeling that she was making fun of him.

'You have to be immortal,' said Mistra. She laughed again. Her eyes gleamed with a green brightness. Her face was alive and warm with life and excitement.

Stephens scowled. It was evident he would not get a satisfactory answer from her without himself coming more into the open. 'Look,' he said flatly, 'What about those books in there? What is the secret of the Grand House?'

For a long time Mistra gazed at him steadily. Her color was a little high, and her eyes abnormally bright. At last she said: 'I thought I heard you in the library. Just how much did you read?'

'Nothing, just now.' Stephens told her about the books he had taken from Tezlacodanal's apartment. She nodded, a thoughtful expression in her eyes, then:

'Those pages,' she said, 'were missing from my copies also, when I got them.'

'And the crossed out words?'

She nodded. They drank in silence for a minute, while Stephens had the impression she intended to say more. She did.

'I happen,' she said, 'to know the names that were blacked out. They are all names that were taken by our little' – she laughed and looked at him questioningly, then finished – 'cult.'

Stephens nodded slowly. He was finding it hard to think.

'So that's it,' he said finally. His voice sounded thick.

'That's it.'

He saw that she was refilling his glass. He watched her with an owlish intensity until she finished, then took a drink.

'What the hell,' he said vaguely, 'is the matter with California? Nutty cults everywhere you look.' Anger surged through him. 'This so-called early Mexican civilization,' he said. 'If ever there was a people that lost its soul, they were it.'

Her eyes, watching him, were as bright as jewels. Her face, however, seemed blurred, as if it were a little out of focus. Stephens went on grimly:

'Of all the bloodthirsty civilizations, the ancient Mexicans really took the cake. Toward the end, more than fifty thousand religious human sacrifices a year were offered to as filthy a crew of gods and goddesses as ever were spawned by the imagination of ignorant men. Bloody devils! Loathsome, diseased minds! Scum of the earth.'

He saw that his second glass was finished. He climbed unsteadily to his feet, hanging onto the bar. He said: 'Let's not talk about that. Let's talk about you. And no more drinks, please. If I take another sip, I'll be drunk.'

He walked toward her, and took her in his arms. She offered no resistance to his kiss, and after a moment she actually responded. They stood embraced, kissing, for nearly a minute. Then he released her and stepped back. He said in a shaky voice:

'You're the most beautiful woman I've ever met.'

He saw that she was watching him again, expectantly. It seemed to be an invitation. Once more, the embrace was long, and her response all that he could ask for.

But when he stepped away, he staggered, and the room spun. Stephens steadied himself with one hand on the bar, and said accusingly, 'I'm drunk!'

'The word is doped,' she said.

Somehow, he was in the center of the room, swaying, peering at her through the strange dimness that was closing in around him.

'I've drugged you,' Mistra said.

Stephens took an awkward step toward her – and saw the floor coming up to meet him. Crash! The shock of the fall momentarily sobered him.

'But why? What's —'

That was not the last thing he remembered; but it was the last thing he remembered with any clearness.

8

Stephens woke up with sunlight in his eyes. He lay for a long moment staring foggily at the ceiling of a strange room, and then abruptly he realized where he was. He climbed out of bed, and hesitated, remembering. Slowly, he relaxed. He was alive. Whatever her reason for drugging him, it was not dangerous.

His clothes were lying on a chair. He dressed hurriedly, and then peered out of the door of his bedroom. As he had already recalled, there was another bedroom a few yards along the corridor. He tiptoed to it, found the door open, and looked in.

He stood for several seconds staring in at the unawakened Mistra. Her face in repose was amazingly youthful. Under other circumstances, he might have decided that she was younger than he had originally believed. At least five or six years younger. Twenty-four rather than thirty.

But there was a memory in him that she had been restless during the long night and that he had heard her plainly. He couldn't recall whether he had been in the room with her, or in the adjoining room. But several times she had cried out, and many times she had talked of the Grand House.

Most of what she had said had been confused. But some of it he remembered vividly.

It must have burned into his mind as fiercely as the *octli* had seared his throat. He felt shaken by the recollection, and he was about to back away out of sight when he grew aware that her eyes had opened and that she was watching him.

Watching him. Stephens retreated a little, automatically.

Her eyes were changed, sunken, bright. He remembered the strange, gleaming light in them just before he had become too sleepy to remember anything. This was the same.

Suddenly, he knew her age was more than twenty-five, more than thirty. He remembered her mention of immortality. 'The house that is old,' she had said in the dark of night, in a tense excitement, as if hidden layers of her life had unfolded with surging violence and shown her a deadly vision. 'The house that is old, *old*.'

Standing there, Stephens realized finally and beyond doubt the secret of the Grand House.

And felt a chill like death, as he saw that she knew he knew. Her lips were parted now. She half rose in the bed, as if to get closer to him. The covers seemed to melt from around her body. Her eyes were pools of flame in the light of the sun pouring through the window. The muscles of her face looked as hard as the stone features of a sculptor's eidolon, and her body was briefly unbeautiful, so tense it was, so completely rigid.

All in one instant her fierce reaction ended. Her body grew visibly lax. She sank back into the bed. She smiled, and said lazily: 'What's this! Going to sneak out on me?'

The spell was broken. Stephens seemed to rise up from a great depth of fantastical imaginings to a consciousness that he was embarrassed. This young woman was too naturalistic for him.

'No,' he said. 'I'm going to shave.'

It was important now to Stephens to get away from her. There was reality in shaving.

'You'll find shaving equipment,' said Mistra, 'in the main bathroom down the hall.'

In the middle of shaving he remembered suddenly: 'Why, this is Christmas Day.'

But the thought could not hold his interest long. His mind slipped back to Mistra. There was no sound now from her. The whole apartment was quiet, except for his own breathing. In that silence, the thoughts began once more to assume proportions.

He wondered if such an idea, once it got into a man's mind, could ever be forced out again. He finished dressing, and headed for the library.

'What I need,' he thought, 'is to read those books through.'

The History of the Grand House was not in its proper place on the shelf. It was, he discovered after a quick search, not on any of the shelves. Also missing were *The Beginnings of Almirante* and *Tanequila the Bold*.

Stephens stepped back, astounded. It seemed incredible that she would have hidden the books. He was still standing there when he heard her shower go on.

Mistra was up.

Stephens walked through the living room and along the hallway that led to her bedroom. Sunlight was pouring through all the east and south windows, and in that brightness the thought mists that had derived from the night could not maintain themselves. He began to feel foolish. The fantasy of immortality faded. But at the same time there were things he wanted to know.

The bedroom door was open. Stephens knocked, loud enough to soothe his conscience but not loud enough for Mistra to hear above the noise of the running water. Inside, the sound of the shower was thunderous, and he saw that the bathroom door was also open. A mist of steam poured lazily from it.

The rushing of the water ended. There followed a padding of bare feet. Then a pause. Then Mistra, enwrapped in a voluminous robe, whistling softly under her breath, came out of the bathroom. She looked at him with thoughtful, blinking eyes, but she said nothing. She seated herself before a massive vanity, and began to fix her hair.

Stephens waited. The eerie feeling that he had experienced earlier in her presence was returning, not so strong now, nor so blurred, but more personal.

She was, he decided, a beautiful woman in the sense that

beauty derived from good looks, maturity, and confidence. Her blonde hair, her brilliant green eyes, her lean and shapely face made her look at once youthful and intelligent. Her skin was a clear tan and there were bone-lines in her face that gave her a Continental appearance. He doubted if her female ancestors had chosen their mates within a narrowly defined racial limit. There was adventurous blood in this woman, and it probably went back a long way.

He realized that his thoughts had carried him far from his purpose in coming to the bedroom. He grew tense. He began, 'During the night you seemed worried about where the marble of the Grand House was quarried. Does anybody know?'

He could see her face in the mirror, the intent look on it. The eyes of her image shifted, and stared at him with an unhurried speculation. He was just beginning to think she didn't intend to answer when she said : 'So I had some more octli nightmares, did I?' She laughed suddenly, and still laughing added, 'I suppose I really ought to give up drinking the stuff.'

Stephens noted that her laughter was not that of a person who was amused, and that she had not answered his question. He waited until she stopped laughing, then :

'About those quarries —'

He was cut off.

'How should I know?' she said. 'The damned place is more than a thousand years old.'

Stephens persisted, 'I gather from the first paragraph of the book on the Grand House that no one knows who built it, but still there must be clues as to where the stone came from.'

He saw that the eyes of Mistra's image in the mirror were looking at him, and that she was smiling ironically. She said, 'People no longer amaze me when they react the way you're doing. Here you are with most of the clues. You don't seem concerned about my drugging you. I can see from your face and I guess from your questions that my explanations seem reasonable to you. And yet, you continue to fight.'

Stephens had been leaning forward, unconsciously straining for her reply. Now, he drew back into his chair, feeling foolish. Here was a cult that practised an old, bloodthirsty religion. Its members lived under the names of people long dead. It was an esoteric group, amoral and possibly criminal. Almost without being aware of it, he had let himself be drawn into the unnatural atmosphere until, for nearly half an hour, his mind had believed the impossible.

He said slowly, 'Why did you drug me?'

Her answer came without hesitation: 'I disoriented you, to see if I could learn something.'

'I don't understand.'

She shrugged. 'I also wanted to find out if you might be the person the others fear you are.'

It took Stephens a moment to make the proper association. He said in astonishment, 'Who do they think I am?'

She turned and stared at him. 'Haven't you realized?' She sounded amazed. She paused as if undecided, then said quietly, 'Somebody built the Grand House. Who? That's been a great worry all these years.'

The explanation disappointed Stephens. It was the madness again, and he was no longer interested.

Mistra said, 'If you are the – builder – you managed to conceal it from me. However, it won't hurt if the others continue to worry about you.'

That startled him. Because – madness or not – one man had already been killed. Why shouldn't Allison Stephens be eliminated also, if they considered him dangerous? Murdered because some madman thought he was a thousand years old. He said uneasily, 'Who killed John Ford, the caretaker? It is related, isn't it?'

She shook her head, and said earnestly, 'No member of the group is responsible. Our mind reader has checked all fifty-three of us.'

'Fifty-three!' Stephens spoke involuntarily. He hadn't expected such exact information.

Mistra seemed not to hear. 'It appears to be a common murder.' She paused. 'Perhaps it'll come in useful to my purposes; I don't know yet.'

Her purposes! The reference tensed Stephens. This was what he wanted to know. He leaned toward her, not seriously expecting a reply, and asked the question: 'What is – your purpose?'

There was a long silence. Her fingers continued to move over her hair, skilfully. Her image-face in the mirror was thoughtful. Finally, slowly, she reached down, opened a drawer, and took out a single sheet. Without looking at him, she said, 'This is an ultimatum that I am shortly going to deliver by radio to the government of Lorillia. The time limit indicated will apply to the day the message is broadcast. The reference to Mars is for psychological reasons. I want to put enough doubt into their minds to insure that they will evacuate the factories I name. But listen!'

She read slowly and in a clear, firm voice:

To the workers in the atomic project known as 'Blackout' – in exactly two hours your entire plant will be razed by torrents of energy from a spaceship. This attack has been authorized by the people of the planet Mars in the full knowledge that your leaders are planning a surprise atomic assault on the United States of America.

Go home quickly. Do not let anyone stop you from being out of your factories at twelve noon. There is no defense.

Atomic war will not be permitted on Earth!

She looked up, and said matter-of-factly, 'I may change the time, but the rest will stand. What do you think of it?'

Stephens scarcely heard. At first his mind was blank, but slowly he grew tense. 'Are you crazy?' he said at last.

She was cool. 'Very sane, very determined, and to some extent dependent on your help. No one person can overcome a well defended fortress.'

Stephens said wildly, 'If you attack Lorillia, they'll assume it's the U.S., and counterattack instantly.'

She looked at him with pursed lips, then shook her head. 'These people are bold, but cunning; they planned to bomb by surprise, and then deny that they were responsible. You don't understand how terrific an idea that is.'

Stephens said, 'They wouldn't get away with it.'

'Yes, they would.' Her tone was even. 'If the U.S. had its principal cities wiped out, its industrial backbone and its heart would be broken. Who would declare war if the first bombs were dropped on Washington while Congress was in session.' Mistra shook her head, and her eyes glinted. 'My friend, you're not being realistic. I assure you that our group would not have considered leaving Earth for anything less than the danger I've outlined.'

Stephens hesitated; and then he thought, almost blank again: I'm reacting as if I believe they have spaceships, as if —

His gaze lighted on the paper she had in her hand. 'Let me see that ultimatum.'

She held it out, an enigmatic smile on her face. Stephens took it, and after a single glance realized why she was amused.

The message was in a foreign language. He was not familiar enough with Lorillian to identify it definitely, but he presumed that was what it was.

Mistra was speaking: 'This is the cause of the split between the others and myself. They want to dismantle the Grand House and take it away from Earth till the storm is over. I believe that we have a responsibility to Earth – that we cannot continue to use our knowledge for private pleasure as we have before.'

'Where would they go?' After he had asked the question, Stephens realized that he was leaning forward, waiting breathlessly for the answer.

She seemed unaware of his excitement. 'To Mars.' Her tone was casual. 'We have an underground center there, where the house would be safe.'

'Would you all move there?'

'Only during the war.'

Stephens pursed his lips. 'Aren't you being unnecessarily fearful? Even granting Lorillia's intentions, do you think they would waste a bomb on Almirante?'

She smiled grimly. 'No, but if the coastal waters opposite Los Angeles or San Francisco were made radioactive, we'd also be affected. Something like that might interfere with whatever it is in the marble that causes long life. Even those of us who opposed flight realize that that is a chance we cannot take.'

Stephens was about to speak again, when it struck him that she had made an admission. He said quickly, 'Then there were others besides yourself against leaving Earth? Why aren't they helping you in the attack?'

Her lips tightened. 'Tannahill was opposed, naturally. Here, he is the legal owner of the house. On Mars, there isn't any state militia to protect his property rights. He would lose the advantage he's held over the rest of us.'

'I see.' Stephens nodded. He could understand Tannahill's dilemma. He frowned finally. 'I don't see how shooting him would break down his resistance.'

'That had nothing to do with it.' She was slightly impatient. 'The solution was more basic than that. The group offered to place itself at his mercy financially. Each individual was to sign over his entire property to the Tannahill estate, and in return was to receive an income. Any person later discovered accumulating money or property would be punished.'

'But that's only money,' Stephens protested. 'If the house can do what you say, then it's priceless.'

'Don't forget the plan was designed to protect the house from possible greater damage.' Mistra made a gesture of dismissal of his argument. 'Oh, it'll work all right. The others were so determined to stick to it that, after Tannahill was shot, they waited till he was out of danger, then went through with the false burial, and proceeded to turn over their holdings to the estate, so that everything would be in readiness for the move the moment Tannahill regained consciousness and signed the release on the house.'

A great light dawned on Stephens. 'I see. Then Tannahill and his uncle are the same? And when he came to, he had forgotten his past?'

'I did that.' She was cool. 'I went to the hospital and drugged him. It caught them by surprise. They thought this was just an argument on an intellectual level.'

Stephens said at that point, 'You – drugged – Tannahill, and destroyed his memory!'

It was not a question. He believed her. In talking to this iron-willed young woman, he had the continual sensation of being beyond his depth. Now, he thought: I'm a legal representative of Tannahill, and I'm listening to this.

He had no thought of using the information against her. He guessed that it was probably unprovable, and besides it was something that must derive from some advanced chemistry. And who would believe it?

Mistra said, 'Actually, the forgetting mechanism of the mind is very easy to interfere with. It can be done at will with deep trance hypnosis. The drug I used is simply more lasting. I can give him the antidote at any time.'

'Why don't the others give it to him?'

'Because,' she said, with a tight little smile, 'they don't know what dosage I gave or what drug I used. Interfering with that *could* do him damage.'

Stephens shook his head wonderingly, but he was still puzzled. He asked, 'But if you didn't shoot Tannahill who did?'

'It must have been a street shooting. The mind-reader established definitely that no one in the group is responsible.'

Stephens remembered the mind-reader's partial failure to read his mind, hesitated, and then said, 'You seem to depend a lot on that mind-reader.' He paused again, reluctant to reveal that the telepath had missed a vital bit of information in his mind. Finally : 'What I'm getting at is, it seems hard to believe that at such a crucial moment, an accidental shooting could have struck down the owner of the Grand House. Was no one else opposed to leaving Earth?'

'One other, besides myself. But he changed his mind when Tannahill did.'

'He *apparently* changed his mind, you mean.'

'Triselle cleared him.'

'Triselle – that's the name of the telepath?'

'Yes.' She broke off, 'Don't underestimate the danger from an accidental shooting. That kind of thing is our nightmare. Wrecks. Drunk drivers. Firebugs. Gang shootings. War.'

'Still —' Stephens hesitated, and then stood up without finishing his thought. He said, 'All this talk about Tannahill makes me feel that I'm being derelict in my duty. I'd better call him – even if it is Christmas Day.'

Mistra turned and stared at him. Her expression was one of amazement. 'Christmas Day!' she echoed. 'That drug really hit you, didn't it? This is the 26th. Don't you remember?'

'The *what*!' said Stephens.

After the first shock had faded, he strained to bring back the memory. Nothing came except what he had already recalled. He remembered a long night broken only by an awareness of Mistra and her cries.

He groaned inwardly.'Now, I'd better phone, and fast.'

He hurried out to the living room, where he had seen a telephone. He called Tannahill first, mentally framing his apologies. None was needed. Tannahill said :

'I was just about to phone you, Stephens. I'm bringing over somebody I want you to meet. We'll be there in about an hour. Hope you had a good Christmas.'

Stephens said that he had, explained that he was not at home but that he would be shortly, and rang off, relieved. Tannahill had sounded calm. Apparently, nothing unusual had happened.

He began to feel a lot better. He dialed his office, heard the receiver lifted, and heard his secretary's voice said, 'This is Almirante 852.

Stephens began, 'Miss Chainer, I want —'

He was cut off. 'Oh, Mr. Stephens, I'm so glad you called. There's been a murder. Mr. Jenkins, the elevator man, was murdered on Christmas Eve.'

9

'Murdered!' Stephens echoed. And then he was silent. Could this be related? Indirectly, Jenkins was a Tannahill employee. Just how he fitted into the vast picture that was beginning to shape up was hard to imagine. And yet – first a caretaker killed, now an elevator man.

Somebody was acting in a grim and decisive fashion. If not the group, then who?

He began to ask questions. The known facts, it turned out, were few. Jenkins had been found beside the elevator with a knife wound in his back. Since there was considerable ground for domestic jealousy, his wife had been arrested and was being held as a material witness.

By the time he had the available details, Stephens was feeling badly. He had liked Jenkins.

'Look,' he said finally, 'I'll be in later today. Good-bye for now.'

He hung up and sat frowning. Things were happening. Where they would lead was not clear. But from what Mistra had said, the group did not attach importance to the murder of the caretaker, except insofar as it affected Tannahill.

It might not occur to them that the death of Jenkins had any relation. Possibly it didn't, but that had yet to be proved. Stephens consciously felt himself to be in a key position to prove it, and prove many other things as well.

He walked back along the hall, knocked on Mistra's door and entered after a moment's wait. Mistra looked at him questioningly, and Stephens explained that he had to leave for an interview with Tannahill. He finished anxiously, 'What about you?'

'I'll be all right.' She sounded casual.

'Perhaps you could come along.'

'No.' She was cool. 'It was getting in here I was worried about. As I told you before, I'm safe now.'

Stephens hesitated, struck by the fact that he still didn't know what she had feared. He said, 'Why was getting in hard?'

'Because,' said Mistra, 'they don't want me to have a ship.'

Stephens parted his lips to speak, closed them again, and then changed his mind. 'Ship!' he said. He felt baffled, and – curiously – reluctant to pursue the matter further. He said, 'I could come back here later, and escort you in or out.'

'Thanks.' Her tone was indifferent. 'But I won't be here.'

It seemed to Stephens, ruefully, that he was receiving just about the most thorough brush-off of his life. He stared at her curiously. 'Aren't you afraid I'll tell somebody what you've told me?'

'And have people think you'd gone mad.' She laughed.

Still, he was reluctant to go. 'Will I see you again?'

'Perhaps.'

Stephens said good-bye, and walked out of the bedroom, half hoping that she would call him back or call a friendly farewell. She didn't. He opened the two outer doors then and shut them behind him. The elevator took him down to the street floor, and presently he was outside blinking up at an early afternoon sun.

His watch had stopped, but he guessed it was one o'clock.

He arrived at his bungalow without further incident.

Tannahill arrived less than ten minutes later, alone. Stephens opened the door to him and realized with a start that this was their first daylight meeting. And yet he would have recognized the other anywhere. A pale, slim young man with hollow cheeks, who walked with the aid of a cane – the picture in the newspaper combined with what he had seen in the darkened cemetery to make the identification easy.

Stephens offered a helping hand, but Tannahill brushed it aside. 'We decided to come separately,' he said, 'so I arrived early.'

He did not explain who the person was he had said he would bring with him, but limped into the living room and sat down. Stephens studied him as unobtrusively as possible. He was trying to imagine him as he had been before he had been shot. Tanequila the Bold, the steely-minded captain of a seventeenth-century Spanish vessel hundreds of years old. It seemed unreal, for this man was bewildered and unhappy. It had to be unreal.

Tannahill looked down at the floor, drew a deep breath, and said, 'I have to confess, Stephens, you got more out of me the other night than I intended to give to anyone. It sort of places a pressure on me to tell you more.'

He paused and looked expectantly at Stephens, who shook his head, and said, 'I can only repeat: I have your interests at heart.'

Tannahill went on, 'I'm going to tell you something I had determined to keep as the deepest secret of all.' He stopped again, then: 'Stephens, I have memories of being in a coffin.'

Stephens waited silently. It seemed to him that even one word might break the spell. Tannahill said, 'I'd better hurry, or we'll be interrupted.'

In a few words, he told how he had been removed from the hospital bed, taken by spaceship for a long distance, buried alive, and, finally, returned to the hospital.

Tannahill's voice ceased, and there was silence in the large living room of Stephens' bungalow. Stephens hesitated, then: 'What floor were you on? In the hospital?'

'When I finally woke up, I was on the fifth. Before that, I don't know.'

Stephens nodded, frowning. 'We could check,' he said. 'It would be interesting if you were lowered out of a fifth story window. The problem would be, how did they do it?'

He would have liked to ask about the ship, but that

seemed too dangerous in view of what he knew. He felt strangely reluctant even to think of the possibility of space-ships and yet an immortal group could be technologically advanced enough to have gotten the jump on the rest of the world. He realized he was still believing all that Mistra had told him.

The sound of a car brought him out of his preoccupation. The machine turned into the driveway, and shifted audibly into medium gear to climb the small hill that led up to the house. Stephens glanced questioningly at Tannahill, who said hastily:

'When I was in Los Angeles, I hired a detective. That must be him now. How much shall I tell him?'

'A detective!' said Stephens. It was the last thing he had expected, and he had a sense of disappointment. It did seem to prove that Tannahill's story was true – but the dis-appointment continued. He answered Tannahill's question cautiously, but actually without interest.

'Depends,' he said, 'on what he's like.'

The car outside was silent now. Footsteps sounded on the gravel, and then climbed the steps. The doorbell rang. A moment later, Stephens was being introduced to a small, sturdy looking man.

'Bill Riggs?' Stephens echoed the name.

'Bill Riggs,' agreed the befreckled individual.

It was scarcely a name one could miss. Stephens shook the other's extended hand, and then stood by lackadaisi-cally, as Riggs said:

'Both of you will have to listen to me for a minute, and see how I size up.'

Tannahill nodded, but Stephens was not interested. He listened with vague attention as Riggs gave his background. He braced up for a few moments when Tannahill turned to him, and said, 'Well, what do you think, Stephens?'

Stephens said, 'Did you know Mr. Riggs before you hired him?'

'Never saw him before in my life.'

It made Riggs a remote, objective figure unconcerned

with local issues. If he could find the person who had written the note to Howland, he might even be valuable. 'I think,' said Stephens, 'you'd better tell him everything.'

Tannahill accepted that, apparently without reservations. He paused once to ask Stephens to quote the contents of the note the district attorney had shown him. And when he reached the point of his subsequent discovery that the date of the burial of Newton Tannahill coincided with his own absence from the hospital, his voice grew hesitant. But he told it.

When the story was finally finished, Riggs said, 'What about fingerprints?'

Stephens hesitated. If Mistra's account were true, it might be that the fingerprints would actually match. He said, 'So far none has turned up.'

Riggs nodded, and said slowly, 'If this thing comes to trial, try to stay clear of that amnesia stuff as much as possible. It's common enough, but in a murder trial it sounds awful fishy.' He broke off: 'Well, I guess it's up to me to get busy.'

He turned toward the door, then faced them again. 'Naturally,' he said slowly, 'I made some inquiries about you down in the town, cautious and casual, of course. I learned that the Tannahills own about a quarter of California, but I discovered, like you told me, that you are practically unknown in Almirante.'

He paused. Tannahill said, 'Yes?'

'Well, sir,' said Riggs, 'not being known is bad. The first reaction that people have to a guy with money is envy. They've got to sort of feel a community of interest with him. My advice is, dish out some of the dough you've got. Make people think they're going to share your good luck. Then if a trial should come along they'll be looking at the thing from the point of view that their profits are being interfered with.'

Tannahill glanced at Stephens, who nodded and said, 'It's a good suggestion. I'd start spending money immediately, Mr. Tannahill.'

Riggs opened the door, and then turned again. 'I'll phone you,' he said, 'first clues I get.'

From the window, Stephens watched the detective's old sedan come into sight on the paved driveway below, then swing around a clump of bushy trees and disappear. The meeting had left a better impression on him than he had anticipated. 'I think we've got a good man there,' he said.

Not until he had spoken did he realize how unconsciously he had used the plural 'we'. It was a good remark to make, just what might be expected of a loyal attorney. And yet it meant that some part of his brain was trying to pretend that life could go on as before.

It couldn't, of course. He had been told that there was a house in which human beings could live forever. If so, he could see that the legal ownership of the Grand House was of basic importance. In striking at the registered owner, Mistra had dislocated the entire pattern of existence of the immortal group.

Tannahill was speaking: 'Stephens, will you call the Ilvers Employment Agency and find out if they've got anyone for me yet.' He broke off: 'Where's your kitchen? I need a drink of water.'

Stephens directed him, and then called the agency. A man's voice answered, and Stephens said, 'I'm calling for Mr. Tannahill —' He got no further.

'Oh, then maybe you could take a message. This is Ilvers speaking. Tell Mr. Tannahill I've got a housekeeper for him.'

Stephens took the full message. It appeared that the help would be up on the 28th for an interview, and the agency man was sure they would be satisfactory. He had been most fortunate in finding two such experienced servants.

Stephens was hanging up when Tannahill came in. Stephens gave him the gist of the conversation. Tannahill nodded, and said, 'My idea is to have dinner downtown, then start on a binge where every drink is on the Tannahill bank account.' His sallow cheeks brightened with color. 'Frankly, I need something like that myself. Care to come?'

Stephens shook his head. 'I'd better stay here and try to get through to Peeley. If I get in touch with him, I'll follow the trail of bottles and see how you're getting along.'

He waited till the other had departed, glanced at his watch, groaned – it was after three – then quickly phoned the telephone company. There was a long pause, and then the operator said, 'You placed a person-to-person call, Mr. Stephens. We have been through to Mr. Peeley's house and office several times, but he himself is not available. Would you like to talk to somebody at his home?'

'Well – yes!' said Stephens.

Half a minute went by, and then a man who identified himself as a servant said, 'Mr. Peeley has gone to the desert for the holidays, sir ... No, sir, we don't know his address yet. That's been the trouble ever since your first call came through ... Mr. Peeley said he would get in touch with us, but up to this hour he hasn't done so. We have your telegram here.'

Stephens gave instructions that the lawyer be asked to phone 'either Mr. Tannahill or Mr. Stephens' – that was the way he put it – at the earliest possible moment.

The sky was like blue velvet, as Stephens drove into town, the air cool but fresh. There was a new elevator operator at the Palms Building, whom Stephens recognized as the father-in-law of the janitor. The old man had substituted on occasion for Jenkins.

Jenkins' body had been removed shortly after it was found. But Stephens had the janitor point out where it had lain. The corpse had been discovered at the head of the basement stairway behind the elevator. Stephens could not find a single mark or stain either in the basement or in the foyer to indicate that Jenkins had fought for his life.

Disappointed, but conscious that he was only beginning, Stephens went up to his office. He stayed just long enough to get Jenkins' home number. He had a fairly sharp picture of the Jenkins' domestic situation, and since Mrs. Jenkins was in jail, he was curious to see what he might find out. He drove to the address by the shortest route: A poor section of the city ... tall, native palms ... a stucco bungalow.

He rang the doorbell and, when no one answered, made his way down an unkempt stone walk to the back. The fenced-in yard was littered and overgrown with grass. At the far end was a garage, and under a tree on the north side stood a small trailer. A faint streamer of smoke emerged from a metal pipe that protruded from the roof of the trailer. Stephens walked over and knocked on the door.

It was opened by a woman whom he recognized as Madge, one of the cleaning-women of the Palms Building.

The woman gasped when she saw him. 'Why, Mr. Stephens!' she exclaimed.

'I'm looking for Mrs. Jenkins,' Stephens lied.

The thin, drab face took on a smug look. 'She's been arrested. Police think she done the old man in.'

Stephens stared at Madge thoughtfully. He had come intending to make use of her intimate knowledge of what went on in the Palms Building. He mustered his most engaging expression.

'Well, Madge, think she did it?'

Her bright, sharp eyes blinked at him. 'Naw. What'd she want to kill him for? She wasn't the type as could get another man. When you're that type of woman, you've got to be careful.' It was obvious Madge had no such fears herself.

She seemed ready to talk, and since the gossipy Jenkins would have kept nothing from her, it seemed reasonable to hope that she might know something.

'Madge,' he said, 'I want you to think over everything that happened during the days before Jenkins was killed. Try to remember what he said to you. Some little point may be the clue we're looking for.'

Madge shrugged. 'Not much help from me, I don't think, Mr. Stephens. Bill told me about the scream you heard in that Indian office.' She giggled. 'And when Mr. Peeley came in later that night he mentioned that, and —'

'Peeley!' said Stephens.

Thunder rolled in his brain. He caught himself. 'Do you mean Walter Peeley, the lawyer from Los Angeles?'

'Yes, that's the one. He always gives Bill a ten dollar bill when he comes in, and he sure is a swell guy.'

'Yes,' said Stephens absently. 'Yes, I guess he is.'

There was a picture in his mind, multi-faceted and fantastic, but how did it fit?

He remembered how on that first night Tezlacodanal had opened the door of the Mexican Import Company expecting a big man.

Peeley was a big man.

He hadn't thought of Peeley as being one of them, principally – he realized now – because of what Mistra had said about Tanequila's possessive attitude in connection with the Grand House. Apparently, it had been enough for that grim personality that the ownership was vested in him. He had no objection to the others attending to the details of administration.

Stephens said, slowly, 'Listen, Madge, if you remember anything, tell me first. Okay?'

'Sure,' said Madge.

He walked away, wondering why Peeley had murdered Jenkins – if he had. It was unlikely that he would worry about anyone knowing that he was in town. Peeley didn't have to explain his movements to Allison Stephens, or anyone else.

He started again downtown and saw by his watch that it was shortly after five o'clock.

Stephens had dinner in town, and then for more than two hours he sat in his car outside the Waldorf Arms, observing who went in and who came out. He had formed a theory about the residents of the building. They were members of the group who at the moment were not masquerading as respectable citizens. As such, like Mistra they would be identified as they really were.

Altogether, while he watched, five people either emerged from or entered the apartment house. Of the five, Stephens had a good look at two, both white men, both distinguished in appearance, and neither of whom he had previously seen.

He gave up his vigil shortly before nine, and headed for the Palms Building.

He was both disappointed and relieved when he saw that the office of the Mexican Import Company was dark. He listened at the door until he was certain, then used his pass key to get in. Bold now, he clicked on the light, verified that he was alone in the place, and immediately located the book that contained the addresses, though not the names, of people with whom the Mexican Import Company did business. He wrote down twenty-two in addition to those he already had. That done, he turned one of the clay figures on its side and he was wondering how he would penetrate to the mechanism inside when a sound distracted him. He turned hastily – and jumped to his feet. A man was standing in the doorway regarding him. The stranger was tall and well-built, and looked sensationally familiar. Yet it took a moment for the identification to sink in.

The man was wearing a mask of the face of Allison Stephens. Stephens had the feeling of looking in a mirror – and then the lights went out.

10

He woke up in darkness. He seemed to be lying on a bare, earth floor. Stephens fumbled cautiously around him with his hands. And there was no doubt. Ground.

Lying there, he remembered that he must have been knocked unconscious from behind.

He stiffened with the recollection, and felt the back of his head. But he could find no bruise, nor was there an area that was sensitive to the touch. Puzzled, he climbed to his feet, and searched for his automatic. To his relief, it was in his pocket. Quickly, he hunted for, and located, a book of matches. The first flame flickered and went out so quickly that he saw nothing. He cupped the next one, and had a brief glimpse of bare earth above and to either side as well as below. Ahead was shadow.

A cave.

The match went out, and he was in darkness again. He thought with concentrated determination: 'I can't be very far from the Palms Building.'

That reassured him briefly. He lit a third match, and this time saw that there was darkness behind as well as in front of him. He also glanced at his watch; the time was five minutes to ten. The match flickered and snuffed out. Stephens started in the direction he had been facing. He moved slowly, balancing himself against one wall, stepping forward gingerly and making sure that there was solid ground ahead before he trusted his full weight on it. He realized presently that he was climbing.

For a while that made him feel better. It was at least the logical direction for escape.

Half an hour went by. 'My God!' he thought, 'Where am

I? And where am I going?' He went over in his mind the nature of the terrain above, and then it dawned on him. Why, of course. He was climbing up toward the Grand House. He tried to remember just how far it was, and guessed half a mile.

About an hour later, he realized that he was no longer in the cave proper. He was walking on a carpeted floor. Stephens stopped short, and stood in the darkness listening. No sound. He struck another match, and by its dim light saw that he was in a small room.

There was a sofa in an alcove in one corner, and several odd-looking kerosene-type lamps on a wall table. He tried to open one of the lamps so that he could light it, but the chimney seemed immovable and he only succeeded in wasting several matches. Fumbling over the smooth surface of the bowl in the darkness, he touched a button.

He pressed on it, and then stepped back in surprise as the core of the lamp glowed brightly. The whole room lit up as if it were daylight.

Stephens would have liked to pause and examine the light, but he was too tense, too aware of the fact that he had been brought here, and that there must be a purpose behind the action.

In a lightning glance, he noted that there were three French-type chairs in addition to the sofa, as well as odds and ends of furniture. More important, when he looked behind a curtain he saw that it opened into a narrow corridor. Carrying the lamp, Stephens followed it to a flight of steps. At the top of the steps was a blank metal wall.

Stephens pushed against it, searching for a lock mechanism, but in the end returned to the room, and examined it again, more carefully this time.

There was no sign of recent occupancy. Dust was everywhere. The colors of the tapestry-covered sofa were dulled by the heavy dust and a copy of *History of the Grand House* lay on it. As Stephens picked up the volume, a sheet fell out. It was covered by fantastic designs, and across the top of the page was written, in faded ink:

Better translate this. The language is growing dim in my mind.

That recalled the thoughts he had had when he had first glanced at the history. In a daze of interest, he sank down on the sofa. The book was open at a chapter titled, *The Saving of the House.*

At first, as he read, he was restless, but slowly his jumpy nerves settled down. He became fascinated, then he forgot himself. The Spanish expedition which made a land journey from Mexico to the vicinity of San Francisco Bay missed seeing the Grand House as the result of a bold action by Tezlacodanal. The Indian had gone down to meet the group. Without hesitation he denounced the party's Indian guides as agents of the wild killer tribes, and offered to lead the expedition along the coast. His ready command of the Spanish language intrigued de Portala who had already been appointed governor of both Californias, and that rather stupid man proceeded to impose such trust in his new guide that he never once suspected the truth. The large party, with its military escort, was led inland, then back again to the coast, when the Grand House was well behind them.

The return journey followed the same route, and so the owners of the Grand House had time to decide finally what they were going to do.

Plastering the house with clay, and planting trees in front of it had saved it from being observed from the sea. But now a more drastic and permanent solution was necessary, to save it from being seen by the Spanish adventurers and priests who would come in ever greater numbers.

It was decided that the house must seem to be destroyed.

Strong guards were posted at all the trails leading to the house. The Indians of the village suddenly found that they were no longer permitted to climb the hill. Hundreds of workmen were brought in from the north, and lived in guarded bunkhouses at night. During the daytime, the women and men of the house, armed and alert, watched the laborers while they carried huge quantities of earth from the east hill – and buried the house.

Buried it completely, and continuously transplanted trees in front of it, and so kept the entire operation hidden from below. The burial required a year and two months, at the end of which time the workmen were returned to their homes. They were back at their homes no more than a day when a well-organized army of wild Indians swooped down upon them out of the hills, and massacred every man, woman and child. There was no suggestion in the book that the attack had been contrived by the Tannahills, but the massacre was very timely. In a single blow it wiped out all outsiders who knew that the Grand House had been buried.

Late one evening, shortly afterwards, the inhabitants of Almirante woke to see a huge fire on the mountain. It burned nearly all night, and in the morning when they were permitted to approach, they saw great slabs of marble lying on the ground covered with soot, and everywhere was evidence that the Grand House had indeed burned down.

A flimsy Spanish hacienda was erected on top of the house. More trees were planted. And Tanequila went down to Mexico City, and gave a number of lavish parties for officials there. He did not remain long enough to arouse envy, but he secured a land grant of vast proportions from a governor who liked his food served daintily. The grant was duly registered in Madrid, and was among those ratified in later years by the American government.

Stephens paused, and he was mentally picturing a hard-eyed Tannahill playing host to people dead these two centuries – when he realized what he was doing. Actually sitting here reading. He thought in amazement: 'Why, I'm taking this situation for granted.' Swiftly, he went back in his mind over what had happened, seeking to discover what had relaxed him. The book?

It seemed to be the answer. The book established the connection of the cave with the Grand House. This was a part of what had gone before. For some reason a member of the group had carried him into this secret cave, intending him apparently to discover this room. Why? And where had the man gone?

Stephens' mind faltered at that point. He could not imagine any valid reason. Abruptly tense, he listened. There was no sound. A great silence pressed around him. He crammed the book into his coat pocket, picked up the lamp, and stood undecided. Which way?

He finally pushed aside the curtain and, stumbling in his anxiety, followed the narrow corridor that led up a flight of steps to the apparently blank metal wall which he had previously examined. He set the lamp down; and he tugged and strained against the wall. After a minute, he was perspiring freely, but he persisted; and, suddenly, an entire section folded noiselessly up.

The rays of the lamp revealed a long room beyond the opening. In the first glance, Stephens saw glass cases and several clay figures similar to those in the Mexican Import office.

Stephens picked up the lamp, and cautiously ventured into the room. The silence was all-enveloping as it had been in the cave, which emboldened him. The room was bigger than he had thought, and at one end was a staircase leading up. He hurried toward it along an aisle between two rows of glass cases. The cases seemed to provide display space for a variety of small figurines and odd looking costume jewelry. He guessed that he was in a museum, but he did not pause for a closer look.

And yet, even as he climbed the stairs, there was the beginning of an identification in his mind. A moment later he reached the top of the staircase, and looked along the gleaming hallway of the Grand House.

Stephens walked slowly forward. Through the double doors, he could see that it was still dark outside. That relieved him considerably. Despite what his wrist watch had indicated, he had been keenly aware of the possibility that it might be morning and not night. Apparently, he had been unconscious only a few minutes.

He glanced into the living room, and then into a book-lined room and, farther back, a bedroom. They were unoccupied, and there was no sound from anywhere. It seemed scarcely the moment to linger in the Grand House. Stephens hurried down the stairs and through the museum. He paused to test the entrance to the cave, to see how it worked from the house side. And then he had closed the panel behind him, and was once more in the cave.

He did not stop now, but walked swiftly through the little room, and so on into the broad reaches of the cave. He was tense again, but determined. He had time to explore the cave, and he intended to do so.

Down he went, and came up presently to where a second and smaller tunnel split off to the right. Stephens glanced at his watch. A quarter after twelve. Unwise to go off on side trips. And yet—

He went. He followed that side tunnel and, with the brilliant glow from the lamp to light his way, half-ran along a cave that gradually curved down and back toward the Grand House, except that he was probably several hundred yards below the level of the house.

The cave ended at a cross tunnel. Stephens glanced along the new underground corridor, first in one direction and then the other. Once again it was a question of which direction he should go. He was standing there uncertainly when the gleam of the wall opposite him attracted his attention. He walked over, and touched it. Metal.

It was dull in color, and he remembered that he had thought it was rock. He strode a hundred yards to where the metal curved away and the cave ended in a blank wall.

Several times, coming back to his starting point, Stephens pushed against the metal, but its somewhat pock-marked surface did not yield. He walked about a hundred and fifty yards past the cross tunnel, and then came to the end of the metal and the tunnel in that direction also.

Once more, he returned to his starting point, and walked back toward what he regarded as the main tunnel. When he reached it, he followed it downward till he came suddenly to a metal wall that spread across the full width of the cave. He pushed at it, convinced that there must be a way through, and that on such a narrow front he might find it. But it was not until he tried sliding it that a section glided smoothly out of position, tilted out toward him, and then rolled noiselessly to the left, revealing a wide opening.

He walked forward – into the sub-basement of the Palms Building.

For several moments, Stephens stood listening. Then he switched on the electric light and shut off the lamp. He examined it briefly, using the one button to light it and turn it off alternately. Satisfied, finally, that its operation was simple enough, he carried it back into the tunnel, and set it down on the dirt floor.

Quickly now, he slid shut the metal door, and noticed that on the inside it was smeared with concrete so that it matched perfectly the concrete base of the building. He opened and shut it several times, and then he headed up to the Mexican Import office.

Everything was as he had left it. The door stood open. The light was on. The clay figure lay on its side.

11

It was nearly one o'clock when Stephens set out to look for Tannahill.

He found the heir and a large crowd of happy young people in a night club called Drink Haven. A waiter thrust a glass into Stephens' hand. 'It's all right,' he said cheerfully. 'It's on the Tannahill millions.' The great, dim room murmured with pleasure. As Stephens pushed slowly nearer Tannahill, who sat in a booth opposite the door, he heard snatches of conversation: '... Do you know, the bill over at' – Stephens didn't get the name of the bar – 'was eight hundred and ninety-six dollars...' '... Somebody told me he gave the waiters fifty dollars apiece...' '... They say the Tannahills used to give week-long festivals ... I sure hope that comes back...'

Somebody jostled Stephens. He looked around. It was Riggs, who said, 'Just thought I'd let you know I'm around. Be seeing you.' He moved off.

Stephens tagged along behind Tannahill to the next bar. The manager met them at the door, and it was obvious that he had had advance notice. In a clear voice, he introduced Tannahill to the largest and most packed lounge Stephens had seen in a long time. After the introduction, there were at least a dozen successful attempts by young women to kiss Tannahill.

Tannahill seemed to enjoy it. Stephens, in the background, could hardly blame him. A man who had been in a hospital for so long must have plenty of steam to blow off. He decided to make no attempt to get near his client, but to go along with the party until he grew tired.

He was on the point of going home about an hour later,

when a woman with jet black hair and a full though not unpretty face squeezed into the booth beside him. She was small, and she wore a flaming red dress. A huge ruby hung from each of her ears. Her fingers glittered with diamond-like and emerald-like rings. There were jeweled ornaments pinned to her dress. She said:

Mr. Tannahill sent me over, and wants you to make the final arrangements.'

Stephens blinked at her. She laughed a trilling laugh.

'I have seen the house,' she said, 'and I will need three girls at least, to begin with. We will have to find some place outside the house for them to sleep. But I will sleep inside. Is that satisfactory?'

Housekeeper! The slight haze of liquor cleared from Stephens' brain. This was the woman mentioned by the placement service man. He remembered how anxious Tannahill was to get servants.

'If Mr. Tannahill approves,' he said, 'you're hired. When can you start?'

'Mr. Tannahill wants me to start tomorrow morning, but I can't make it until the day after. That will have to do.' She spoke very firmly.

'You mean the 29th?'

'Mr. Tannahill offered me a hundred dollar bonus if I would start tomorrow, and fifty if I started on the 29th.' She laughed gaily. 'I will take the fifty.'

It was two o'clock when he learned that her name was Gico.

Gico Aine.

It took Stephens a little while to recall where he had seen the name before: In *Tanequila the Bold*, there had been a a paragraph which, as he recalled it, had stated: 'Alonzo was the unlucky one. His mistress, an Indian woman named Gico Aine, stabbed him to death.'

Stephens was still thinking of the implications when he got home about four. So the gang was trying to get back into the Grand House, one way or another.

It was broad daylight when Stephens woke to the sound

of dishes rattling in the kitchen. He blinked, momentarily had the illusion that it was his housekeeper; and then, realizing that couldn't reasonably be so, climbed out of bed and into his dressing-gown.

He stopped in the kitchen doorway. Mistra Lanett was standing on a footstool before an open cupboard door. She glanced around and looked at him calmly.

'I'm making breakfast,' she said.

Stephens felt his pulses leap. He stood like that for a few seconds, trembling with excitement. And then he had control of himself again.

He eyed her warily. This woman had more power over him than he cared to think about, since from her viewpoint their relation was probably intended to be no more than a casual one. He walked slowly forward. He said:

'This is a quick reappearance of a young lady who said that she might *perhaps* see me again. What have you in mind now?'

She was reaching up to the top shelf. While he watched, she brought down some dishes, and then turned toward him, a faint, teasing smile on her face. 'What's the matter? Didn't you want to see me again?'

He was too experienced to permit a woman to tantalize him with a flirting approach. He stepped forward, and caught her roughly in his arms. He could feel her yielding body against the thin flannel of his pajamas. Her lips waited for his, but did not return the pressure he gave them. He let her go finally, and said stiffly, 'You were able to leave the Waldorf Arms without trouble?'

She nodded. 'I took the ship up about a hundred miles and came down in a lifeboat.'

It was an unexpected reply.

'You have spaceships?' he said.

Mistra was setting the table. 'You were in one.' She spoke without looking at him.

Once more, her words reached too far for him to follow quickly. He stared at her, feeling irritated; and yet his mind worked furiously, trying to fit her statement in with what he knew. Her apartment was unusually constructed; the building itself, with its dome, was an odd structure. It was a fantastic thought, but no more so than the ones he had already accepted.

'What does it do?' he asked finally. 'Does the dome slide open on a foggy night, and you and your ship soar up into the darkness?' His tone was facetious.

'Strangely enough,' said Mistra, 'that's a very accurate statement of how it works.' She broke off. 'But right now I want you to get dressed. We can talk while we eat. It's very urgent.'

Stephens shaved and dressed and felt inner conflict. It was only as he sat down to a breakfast of French toast, bacon and coffee that his tensions began to relax. Bright-eyed, he looked at Mistra Lanett. Her eyes were serenely green; her hair done up rather primly; her face —

There he paused, remembering the mask he had found in her purse. The fact that she had carried a different 'face' with her seemed to suggest that, as Mistra Lanett, she was herself. He saw that she was watching him, her cheeks crinkled into a smile. It seemed unlikely that a mask could be so sensitive to every changing expression.

He said curiously, 'What is the secret of immortality?'

Mistra shrugged. 'The Grand House.'

Stephens persisted, 'But how does it affect the body?'

'The skin cells de-differentiate,' she said.

Stephens echoed the unusual word, and then looked at her questioningly.

She explained: 'The skin cells actually return to their youth. It affects the whole body, organs, everything. Well' — she hesitated — 'almost to their youth. We do age, very slowly.'

Stephens shook his head. 'How do you mean, return to their youth? What about the rest of the body?'

Her tone was suddenly indifferent. 'The secret of youth is in the skin. Keep the skin young, and time is conquered.'

'You mean, all these cosmeticians with their emphasis on beauty of the skin have actually got something?'

She shrugged. 'Any beneficial treatment of the skin is good. But the process of de-differentiation is more fundamental than the surface care you can give yourself. You've heard of these life-forms that can grow new arms or legs. That's de-differentiation, and it's the skin that does it.'

She broke off, said, 'I can tell you more about that some other day. Right now I'm pressed for time. I need a lawyer.'

Her expression was suddenly earnest, her eyes narrowed. She leaned toward him. 'Mr. Howland called me yesterday afternoon. He wants me to come to his office before noon today for an interview as a witness in the murder of John Ford, the caretaker of the Grand House, I ought to have a lawyer to come with me.'

Her explanation struck a chord of excitement in Stephens. Sharper than before, he pictured the predicament of these people. First, the group as a whole frustrated by the fact of Tannahill's ownership of the house. Now, Mistra compelled to tell her story – some story, anyway – to a representative of the law. Theoretically, of course, she could escape by putting on a mask and assuming a new identity. But that could have other legal repercussions; any transaction that involved transferring property or money from one individual to another sooner or later came under the scrutiny of a government official, even if it was only the tax collector. Surely, a lawyer could gain an advantage somewhere in all this!

Mistra said, 'Will you represent me?'

Stephens emerged from his reverie, and said, 'Why – I guess so. But wait!'

He sat frowning. As the local agent of the estate, could he agree to represent anybody connected with the case without consulting Tannahill? He said, temporizing, 'Just where do you fit into the murder?' He added, quickly, 'I know some of these things vaguely, but tell me from the beginning.'

'I was secretary of the late Newton Tannahill, and I was up at the house until a few weeks ago when I quit for personal reasons. That's the gist of it.'

'Was that the last time you saw John Ford?'

'I saw him once on the street about a week ago.'

'I see,' said Stephens. He nodded decisively. 'I'll surrender you for questioning,' he said, 'but I don't guarantee to represent you if there is a trial. It might not be ethical for me. We'll have to figure out a detailed story, of course, that you can tell Howland and' – sardonically – 'in view of your background, it had better be plausible.'

Mistra said, 'I'll tell you about myself.'

Stephens listened with absorption. The account began five years before when she had entered Newton Tannahill's employ. She recounted the nature of her duties. She had been hired to catalogue and arrange her employer's art collection, but later her work became more general until finally, during his frequent absences, she was in complete charge of the house and its immediate grounds.

A major omission in her story was her failure to explain how she, who had needed a job a few years before, now wore mink coats and drove big cars. Nor did she give any clear reason why she had resigned her position suddenly two weeks earlier. They were questions which Howland would be sure to ask.

Stephens asked them also.

'My money!' Mistra said, as if it was a new thought. 'Oh, I made investments on Mr. Tannahill's advice. He was an astute speculator.'

'And why did you quit the job when you did?'

'I had stayed on because of loyalty to Mr. Newton Tannahill,' she said. 'Naturally, that obligation wouldn't apply to his heir.' Her expression was bland.

Stephens thought for a moment, then nodded. 'Sounds all right,' he said. 'Are you sure there's nothing that could backfire on you?'

She hesitated; then shook her head. 'Nothing that Howland could find out about.'

Stephens said, 'I'll call the district attorney, and maybe I can get a postponement.'

'I'll wash the dishes,' said Mistra.

Stephens watched her for a minute as she briskly cleared the table. He liked the coziness of the scene. On impulse, he grabbed at her arm as she passed him. She evaded him. 'You make that call,' she said in a mock-severe tone.

Stephens laughed good-humoredly, stood up, and presently was dialing Howland's number. The secretary put him through at once and it was quickly clear that the district attorney would not consider a delay.

'I've got to have her down here this morning. I'm not fooling, Stephens.'

Stephens said slowly, 'Aren't you being a little high-handed? After all, the lady is available at any time.'

Howland spoke curtly, 'If she isn't here by noon today, I'll have to issue a warrant for her, Stephens.'

Stephens did not try to hide his amazement. 'I protest such sharp treatment. But if you insist, we'll come.'

'I insist,' Howland said. 'But now, if you don't mind, I'm going to ask you a question.' His voice changed, grew more suave, more confidential. 'About the murder of John Ford, Stephens.'

'Yes?' Stephens waited expectantly.

'Is Miss Lanett your only connection with the case?'

Oh, no you don't! Stephens thought. You're not going to get an admission out of me that we've even thought of such a thing. Aloud, he said, 'What are you getting at?'

'Nobody else has approached you?'

Stephens said, 'Not yet. Have you been recommending me?'

That brought amused laughter. 'Well, hardly.' The laughter ended. 'Seriously, Stephens, somebody's going to be executed for killing that nigger, and it looks like big game. I have reason to believe the murderer has taken alarm, and I thought he might have hired himself a lawyer.'

Stephens said stiffly, 'Then you know who it is, do you?'

'Well, yes, I suppose we do. The problem is to get the evidence and a motive, and then of course there are other angles about which I will say nothing. But now, look, Stephens' – patronizingly – 'you bring that dame in this morning, and everything'll be okay. Good-bye.'

Stephens hung up the receiver, started immediately to dial the number of the Grand House, and then put the phone back on its cradle.

Wait, he thought, till after the interview. I'll have something to tell him then.

Mistra came in as he reached that conclusion and said cheerfully: 'We'll take my car. I'll be your chauffeur today, wherever you want to go.'

Her car was a new Cadillac convertible with a gleaming chartreuse paint job. Stephens looked at its brilliant exterior, and climbed in beside her. He watched her profile as she backed to the highway, and he wondered again: A secretary five years ago – now this! It would be hard to explain.

They reached the courthouse without incident, and were admitted at once to Howland's private office. The district attorney stood up from his chair, and regarded Mistra very deliberately. His gaze shifted over her sleekly-dressed body, down to her costly shoes, up to her mink neckpiece and her expensive hat. A smile of satisfaction spread over his face. Then his mood changed. He said abruptly, 'Miss Lanett, were you the mistress of Newton Tannahill?'

Mistra looked surprised, then amused. 'No!' she said firmly.

'If that is the case,' Howland said grimly, 'how do you explain the fact that every month, since you were first employed, the estate has been paying you $12,000, a total of $144,000 a year, for nearly five years? A considerable salary, you must admit, for a secretary who was originally hired to catalogue an art collection.'

Stephens half-turned to see what Mistra's reaction was. He was thinking, 'Yes, how *do* you explain it?' And then the figures penetrated.

His calm dissolved. He had been like a man dangling over an abyss, uncertain of his position, eager to hold on to what he had and to balance himself somehow through a complex situation. In a curious fashion he had come to believe in

everything. It was all there in his mind, the conviction that
a group of immortal men and women had lived for centuries in an ageless house that stood on a high hill overlooking the timeless ocean. He knew that they had an
advanced science and that they were wealthy.

Abstract knowledge – already it had inspired him to do
things, but only with the top of his mind, thinking in sub-
stantially legal terms.

The naming of her income struck deep. One hundred and
forty-four thousand dollars a year! He was not a man who
normally thought in terms of money. But this hit him hard.

As from a great distance he grew aware that Howland
was saying, '... confident Miss Lanett will realize she must
cooperate with the authorities. I'm sure she never dreamed
that what started out as a unique case of deception would
end in murder. Naturally, she is perfectly aware of what I
am leading up to. Aren't you, Miss Lanett?'

The young woman said, 'I haven't the faintest idea what
you are talking about. And I deny all your charges and
innuendoes whatever they may be. I know nothing about
the death of John Ford.'

Howland looked impatient. 'Come, come, Miss Lanett.
You had better realize your situation. I'm still friendly
toward you. I'm still prepared to make a deal whereby no
charges will be pressed against you for being, say, an
accessory before and after the fact in a conspiracy that has
already resulted in murder.'

Stephens decided it was time for him to speak. He swallowed hard, made a last effort to adjust himself, and said,
'What do you want from Miss Lanett?' He grew calmer,
more in control. He went on: 'In view of your questions, I
would like to know one thing: How did Newton Tannahill
die?'

Howland was looking at Mistra satirically. 'Yes, Miss
Lanett, how did he die?'

Mistra stirred, but spoke casually.

'Heart failure. Doctor de las Cienegas will be able to tell
you better than I. He examined the body when it was in the

undertakers being prepared for burial. And, since that was what I was told, I just took it for granted that that was what the New York death certificate said.'

'Oh, yes,' said Howland. 'The New York State death certificate. Has anybody any idea where it is? Has anybody, in fact, ever seen it?'

He broke off with a wave of his great hand. 'Never mind that now. Miss Lanett!'

There was a pointedness in his voice, that made Stephens sit up. He saw that Mistra had caught the change of tone also. She was stiffening.

'Yes?' she said.

'Have you any objection to meeting Arthur Tannahill, the heir to the estate?'

Mistra hesitated. 'I have no desire to,' she said finally.

Howland pushed himself out of his chair. 'Is it possible,' he said, 'that your reluctance to meet him face to face could have anything to do with the fact that this morning when we opened the grave of Newton Tannahill, we found the coffin empty.'

He came around the desk. 'If you have no great objection,' he said sarcastically, 'we'll drive up to the Grand House right now and I will introduce you to Mr. Tannahill. Shall we go?'

Stephens, who had been thinking of the implications, said quickly, 'I'll call Mr. Tannahill and tell him the situation.'

Howland scowled at him. 'You will tell him nothing. You start trying to warn him, and we'll have a police escort up there.' He grinned. 'I want this to be a surprise.'

Stephens said in genuine anger, 'That's the damnedest thing I ever heard. Are you sure you know what you're doing?'

'Never,' said Howland firmly, 'been more sure in my life.'

Stephens controlled himself, and said in a tense voice: 'For heaven's sake, man, use your head. This is a Tannahill you're planning to treat in this arbitrary fashion. What about fingerprints? Surely, they can be checked and this whole matter settled.'

He felt uneasy the instant he had spoken. If Mistra had told him the truth, then the fingerprints of the uncle and the nephew would logically be the same. It seemed incredible that they had not thought of such a possibility. If they had, then it was unlikely that fingerprints would be available.

Howland said, 'We've checked with all the usual agencies, and none has a record of the fingerprints of Newton Tannahill. Since only official prints would have a legal standing, that is conclusive for us.'

Stephens could not decide whether or not the news relieved him. 'Nevertheless,' he said doggedly, 'let me call Mr. Tannahill and make an appointment. I'm sure we can settle the whole incident without any unnecessary rudeness.'

Howland shook his head. 'To hell with that!' he said thickly. 'Everybody's equal before the law, and there'll be no favorites. Are you coming, or shall I have a policeman hold you here till Miss Lanett and I get up to the Grand House?'

As he preceded the man down the steps a few moments later, Stephens was thinking: 'This is the result of Howland losing the agency for the estate. He's hitting back as hard as he can.'

At least there was one good thing about the situation: For the time being, his own and Tannahill's interests almost coincided.

12

Old was the house. For a thousand years or more it had crouched on its mountain, and looked down at the unchanging sea. And like the sea it had no purpose, no thought, no desire. As the days of the years went by, outward change was wrought upon its basic structure, but only outward change: New decorations, new efforts at cleanliness, new interior arrangements. Again and again the trimmings were renewed and altered. Different designs of gardens were conceived and laboriously achieved to give it an ever greener, more cultivated setting. Masses of earth were moved, landscaped, left for years, and then removed. Trees were planted and lived and died or were felled. The house neither saw nor felt nor cared nor changed. Through all the years it sat solid on the solid earth, a lifeless edifice of marble and mystery.

It was an imposing, single story house, and it stood on a high hill. Stephens had often thought that what saved it from the attention of the people who passed by on the road below was that its most outstanding feature was hidden by a barrier of trees. He had seen the steps on his one trip up to the house years before, and he was still impressed.

As the car climbed higher, he looked back. The sun was shining slantingly down onto a vast body of water that began just west of where the town ended. To the right and left, the suburbs of Almirante spread into a series of hills that were green with growth. Far to the south there was a twin silvery gleam where the railway came out of the brush and concealing valleys and turned gradually to the Pacific.

The car made a sharp turn around a clump of trees, leveled off on the knob of the mountain, and there was the house.

The first look brought Stephens upright in his seat. He had forgotten the full effect of the steps. Or perhaps the house hadn't meant so much to him the last time he had seen it. The hedge of trees must have been planted with the deliberate intent of making the memory grow vague.

It hid the steps. Passersby could gaze up over the trees and see what looked like a wide-fronted, one-story house. Not a single step was visible from farther down, and there were (Stephens counted them meticulously) twenty-five steps altogether. They ran the full front of the house, a hundred feet at least, and they reached up to a broad marble terrace which centered on a thick glass double door.

The steps were of marble. The house was made of highly polished slabs of the same material, and its whiteness was an illusion of distance. Seen from nearby, it had a greenish tinge underlying a shiny gray white.

Stephens followed Mistra and Howland out of the car, climbed slowly behind them up to the terrace, and stood by as Howland rang the bell.

A minute, and some five rings later, there was still no reply.

Stephens was the first to leave the door. He walked along the terrace conscious of the house and of the silence. A faint breeze touched his cheeks, and that brought a memory of the shock he had had in Howland's office, and brought the wonder if a thousand years before a woman – still living – had stood here on this undying marble and felt the caress of a similar breeze on just such a timeless California winter afternoon such as this.

It wouldn't have been called California then, of course. That was before the Spaniards with their Baja and Alta California designations, before the Aztecs came, perhaps before even the half-mythical Toltecs.

Stephens gazed into the distance below, where the green

land touched the bright, placid sea ... For almost fifty generations the house had looked from its eminence into those depths, and watched strange men and women come up from the remote, invisible lands beyond the horizon. Stephens felt a sudden melancholy, a deadly envy, a reluctance to grow old and die, while the immortal house continued its vigil here under the eternally warm skies of California.

Gloomily, he peered down over the edge of the marble terrace. The sides of the steps were polished to almost the same smoothness as their surface. But here and there small chips had been broken off. He wondered if they were products of ancient battles: flung stones, the impact of arrowheads.

He forgot that. What was there about this place? How did the house help people to live forever? He knelt, and reaching down, pulled loose one of the marble chips. He put it in his pocket, intending to have it analyzed. As he did so, he turned – and saw that Mistra was standing no more than a dozen feet away. Their eyes met; Stephens looked away shamefacedly, but not before he'd seen that she was amused.

The moment was saved for Stephens when the door opened and Tannahill's voice spoke to Howland. Stephens hurried forward. 'Mr. Tannahill,' he said grimly, 'I wanted to call you, but I was threatened with arrest if I did so.'

Tannahill looked at him, eyes narrowed, then at Howland. 'Better come in, all of you,' he said finally. He added: 'I was taking a nap, and I haven't yet secured any servants. This way.'

Stephens was the last to enter. He found himself in a large center hallway. The floors were brightly polished. There was a stairhead at the far end, that led down to a landing from which the steps went down at right angles out of his line of vision. A dozen oak doors opened off from the hallway, six on either side. It was to the nearest of these doors that Tannahill directed them.

Stephens lingered behind the others long enough to whisper to Tannahill, 'Things are bad.'

Tannahill nodded. 'I expected it.'

In the living room, they all sat down except Tannahill. His gaze fastened on Mistra. 'Ah,' he said, 'my uncle's secretary, Mistra Lanett – the young lady who resigned without notice just before my arrival. Why did you do it?'

Howland interrupted. 'I can give a possible explanation for her action,' he said. 'There is, I think, reason to believe that Miss Lanett was the mistress of – uh – your uncle. A few years ago, she was in effect cast off by him. And what she did to inconvenience you was no doubt her only method of paying back – your uncle.'

Tannahill said, 'Let's stop this song and dance. Have you opened the grave?'

'Yes.'

'What did you find?'

'The coffin was empty.'

'Are you going to lay a charge of murder against me?'

'Yes,' said Howland. 'Yes, I am.'

'You fool!' said Tannahill. But Stephens saw that he had grown paler.

There was a silence.

Stephens did not move or speak. He had no feeling that Tannahill had made a mistake in forcing the issue into the open. No one knew better than he that Howland was on the rampage, and he had an idea the district attorney was surprised at the sharp way in which his purpose had been attacked from the moment they entered the house.

He watched Tannahill limp over to a chair and sink into it. Across from him, Howland leaned back in his chair, looked at Mistra and said:

'Well, Miss Lanett, are you prepared to play ball with my office?'

Tannahill glanced up, too. A touch of color was coming into his cheeks. 'I'd like to ask Miss Lanett some questions.'

Howland said roughly, 'You can cross-examine her on

the witness stand. All I want from her now —'

That was where Stephens interrupted. 'Howland!' He spoke piercingly. 'Let me understand clearly the nature of the charge against Mr. Tannahill. Are you going to accuse him of the murder of his uncle and of John Ford? Or only of John Ford?'

Howland pondered that briefly. 'We'll make our charge at the time of the arrest,' he said.

'I suppose,' said Stephens grimly, 'that the motives of the *former* agent of the Tannahill estate might be misunderstood when, in the capacity of district attorney, he brings charges against his old client. You are prepared to have such a misconstruction placed upon your action?'

It was evident that Howland was not a man who worried about the future too much. He waved one hand impatiently. 'Naturally,' he said, 'the arrest will not be made until our case against Mr. Tannahill is complete. We are waiting verification from the hospital where he convalesced as to his whereabouts on May 3rd of this year. And there are a couple of other things. I warn Mr. Tannahill, however, that he had better make no attempt to leave the city.'

Tannahill climbed to his feet. He looked tired. 'It seems to me that Mr. Howland is making a mistake in trying to get to the top without the support of the local, shall I say, financial interests which I am sure he could obtain if he went at it the right way. One thing I can tell him.' His eyes stared straight into Howland's. 'If he takes the plunge and lays this' – he hesitated – 'this ridiculous charge against me, he'll find himself in a fight where there are no holds barred.'

He finished quietly, 'And now, good-bye, Mr. Howland. I shall no doubt be seeing you again.'

Howland bowed ironically. 'I'm sure of it,' he said. He stood up, and glanced at Mistra. 'Are you coming, Miss Lanett?'

The woman came swiftly over to Stephens. 'I'll drive Howland down, then come back here and pick you up.'

She didn't wait for Stephens to agree. She turned and walked toward the door. She and Howland went out. Stephens looked around, and saw that Tannahill was watching him.

Tannahill and himself and the house – to Stephens for the moment the house was almost as great a factor as the human beings. He sat down and let himself become aware of its moods. No sound came, nor manifestation. The marble house stood quiet through one more day of its long existence, undisturbed by the breathing and the life of its inhabitants. In a thousand years it had proved itself immune to such minor irritations.

Tannahill broke the silence. 'What was that about Howland having been the former agent of the estate?'

When Stephens had explained, Tannahill sat for a long time with his lips pursed; finally: 'Men, generally, do not like to feel that they are being bought. But don't be annoyed if I tantalize Howland by appearing to offer him the local agency again. It won't happen, you understand. Neither Howland nor I would trust each other after this incident. But the possibility of regaining the rather considerable income might have an effect on him where an outright offer would be repulsed.'

Stephens made no comment. He wasn't so sure that Howland wouldn't grab at an outright offer. He said quietly, 'Mr. Tannahill, have you any idea why a man would want to pretend to die, give up a huge inheritance tax, and then move back onto the estate pretending to be his nephew?'

Tannahill said, 'Don't talk nonsense. I have a theory, if that's what you mean. It seems obvious that I was put into the grave because my uncle's body was not available.' He leaned forward, earnestly. 'What other logical explanation can there be? His murder started the whole train of events. Whoever did this had to get him legally buried without any suspicion of murder. So they got my unconscious body out of the hospital and substituted it. Apparently there was a resemblance. Since I was unconscious, I was not expected to remember the incident.'

It was startlingly plausible. Stephens said cautiously, 'We might start building a case on that basis. It's worth trying.'

Tannahill was somber. 'What about Miss Lanett?'

Stephens hesitated, then: 'As your uncle's secretary, she will undoubtedly be a key witness. I'm not so much worried about what she will actually say as about the facts that may be brought out in connection with her position in the house, her obvious wealth, and so on.'

'I see,' said Tannahill thoughtfully.

Stephens was apologetic. 'I'm sorry. Things are certainly working against you.'

Tannahill stood, intent and grim. He said carefully, 'I have an idea what this Lanett woman wants, and I'll do it if necessary.' His voice tightened. 'I want to make it clear to you, Stephens, that there is nothing I am not prepared to do. I learned from reading into the past history of my family that a bold, desperate man does not set limits on his actions in a crisis.'

Stephens wondered how many of the family books Tannahill had read, but he did not press for details. He could hear an automobile climbing the hill and guessed that Mistra was returning. He hesitated, then said, 'Mr. Tannahill, as I see this problem our first job is to try to head off an arrest. To that end, I think we are justified in leaning heavily on local regard for the Tannahill family.'

He explained what he had in mind, and finally finished, 'We'll just have to trust the newspapers will take your side, and will not publish anything that we tell them now. But I do think they should be forewarned, and by us.'

Tannahill, who had listened with evident uneasiness to the plan, said reluctantly, 'You certainly believe in taking direct action.'

'I am also,' Stephens said, 'going to call on Judge Porter and Judge Adams. I have an idea they don't know what Howland is up to.'

He half-believed that. It was possible that the group as a

whole did not know what was building against them. On this point, Mistra could not be trusted. Her bias against Tanequila might keep her from doing anything to save him. Besides, she had her own plans.

Tannahill held out his hand. 'By heaven, Stephens, I like this more every second.'

As they shook hands, Stephens said, 'Our best defense, if the worst comes, will be to produce the murderer ourselves. I'll call you as soon as I have anything to report.'

Stephens paused at the top of the steps of the Grand House and looked around him. Mistra was just turning into the driveway. The breeze was stronger than it had been, and the view almost took his breath away.

The early afternoon sky was brilliantly bright. The Pacific was a mass of short, jewel-like, choppy waves that glinted in the sun. The city below wore its greenest mantle; houses and buildings peeped through the luxuriant plant life.

Mistra pulled up below him, and Stephens started down. As he came level with her, she reached over and opened the door for him. She said, 'Hurry, please!'

Startled by the urgency in her tone and the expression on her face, Stephens scrambled in beside her. 'What's the matter?'

She made no answer except that the long machine leaped forward. She pressed a button, and the convertible top glided up over his head. Windows rolled into position.

Instead of turning around as she came to the end of the main driveway and so on back down the hill, she twisted the machine around a group of trees and along a narrow paved road, that sloped downward between a high hedge. The speed of the car increased so sharply that Stephens said, 'Mistra, for heaven's sake —'

He stopped, and swallowed hard. The road ended a hundred feet ahead at what looked like the edge of a cliff. Stephens turned on Mistra in astounded dismay – and saw that she was holding a transparent shield over her nose and mouth. Simultaneously, he grew aware of an odor in the car.

Gas!

He was still thinking about that vaguely, and fumbling for the emergency brake when the instrument panel bumped gently against his head. The sensation lasted a moment, only; then ceased to exist.

13

Stephens blinked, and heard Mistra say, '... You can tell Mr. Tannahill if you wish to warn him.'

The words seemed meaningless; and Stephens, remembering in a flash the desperate situation of the car racing toward the edge of the cliff, grabbed instinctively again at the emergency brake.

It wasn't there.

Amazed, he looked around him, and saw that he was in Mistra's apartment. To his right was the bar. To his left the corridor that led to the bedrooms, and over to one side there was a window through which the sun was shining. A radio chattered softly in the near corner, and Mistra, who had evidently been bending down behind the bar when he first glanced at it, came up into view holding two glasses.

She stared at Stephens and said, 'I assure you, you can call from here. This phone connects with a relay system and so with the regular telephone lines.'

Stephens glanced at the phone, and then shook his head, unwilling to admit that he didn't know what she was talking about. Twice, he went back in his mind over what had happened, and each time he came to the point where the car had been hurtling toward the edge of the cliff, and he had reached for the emergency, and then —

This!

He looked at her accusingly. 'What did you use,' he said, 'to knock me out?'

Mistra smiled. 'I'm sorry,' she said, 'but there was just no time to explain, and I thought you might struggle with me.'

Stephens said irritably, 'If I remember correctly, you were to take Howland back to his office and —'

Mistra spoke quietly, 'I contacted the group and told them what Howland was planning. It was decided that only one thing mattered now: to cover up. Pressure will accordingly be brought to bear on Howland. But we're all afraid it won't work.'

Stephens thought of all the important people in town whom he believed to be members of the group, and who would be able to apply pressure; and he said sharply, 'Why not?'

Mistra was shaking her head. 'My dear, you don't understand. Howland has political ambitions. If his friends press him too hard, he'll turn on them. It happened once before in our history and we lost control of the town for several years. We don't care to have that happen again.'

Stephens said, 'What does the group plan to do?'

Mistra was brisk. 'First, of course, the attempt will be made to dissuade Howland. If that fails, we've decided to let him have his way. In that case, of course, we'll do our best to ruin him.'

'You mean, let him arrest Tannahill?' Stephens shook his head stubbornly. 'I'm sorry, but I still intend to prevent that if I can.'

'Why?'

'I just can't help but feel,' said Stephens quietly, 'that the woman who drugged Tannahill might not have his interests at heart. And if the group as a whole also dislikes him, then what we have here might not be a rescue at all, but a kind of legalized lynching. Well, I refuse to play along.'

'The group may dislike him,' said Mistra, 'but that has not influenced their judgment. They feel that change of ownership is too complex a process. There are no family heirs, and it is even possible that we will lose the house. I felt I had to take that chance in order to block the group's move to desert Earth, but I was not happy about it.'

Stephens said steadily, 'There's a trick here somewhere. You've admitted that the group is desperately anxious to cover up. Do you swear that they're not planning to sacrifice Tannahill?'

Her reply was prompt. 'I can't swear it, but I believe it, knowing them.'

He had to confess that it was an honest sounding answer. She couldn't possibly speak for the individuals of the group, whose secret intentions were known only to themselves and perhaps to the mind-reader among them.

He said, 'What I'm thinking is that we should try to avoid an unpleasant type of arrest. I believe we should be in a position to surrender Tannahill through his lawyer and be ready to arrange bail immediately. There's no valid reason for Howland having his own way unchecked in this affair.'

Mistra said, 'Then you'd better phone Tannahill. Howland is under pressure right now to lay off. If he reacts as we expect, he'll have that arrest order out in an hour.'

Stephens said, 'What?'

He jumped to his feet, and a moment later he was talking to Tannahill. He explained what was going on without giving his source of information, and then outlined his plan. He finished, 'You must have a service car somewhere on the estate that is not easily identifiable. Take it.' He added, 'If possible, whenever you leave the car, walk without your cane ... grow a mustache – and we can meet as I've suggested.'

Tannahill sounded undisturbed. 'That's good advice, Stephens,' he said, 'and I'll do it.'

Stephens hung up, relieved.

Mistra said, matter-of-factly, 'And now you'd better look out of the window.'

Stephens frowned at her. 'Window!' he said.

The suspicion that came brought him to his feet. The venetian blinds were slanted upward, and sunlight was pouring through them in a blazing abundance. He straightened the blinds, and stopped, swaying. In spite of his anticipatory thought, he felt as if he were going to faint. 'Oh, my God!' he gasped.

The sky was dark. There was immense, hazy distance below.

The initial feeling of shock left him. He saw that the

world below was shapeless and without life. A curious roundness added a final touch of unreality. Finally, he remembered where he had seen similar blurry views: V-2 photographs taken from heights of a hundred miles or more gave that same bizarre effect.

He whirled away from the window, brushed past Mistra, and raced along the corridor that led to the combination library and music room. It was as he remembered it. As he emerged, after one quick look, he saw that the metal door at the top of the stairway – which had been locked on his first visit – was now open. He climbed up into what was unmistakably the control room of a spaceship.

There were four chairs built into frames that were attached to the floor. They were set in a row before a long, low, curving control panel. The chamber was evidently perched on top of the living quarters, for through 'windows' he could look in every direction, and see the curved metal hull of a stream-lined but almost square-built ship. Above the windows, and directly in front of the control chairs were several television-tube surfaces, one of which had a picture on it of the world beneath.

The ship seemed to be floating. There was no sense of movement, nor sound of motors. Stephens started to sit down in one of the chairs but jerked erect as he thought: 'This is definitely her apartment. That domed effect on the Waldorf Arms is necessary because underneath it is the hangar of this ship. She wasn't fooling me about that.'

He felt briefly amazed that he had resisted the idea so long, despite the information that he had. From the beginning, words alone had not been enough to convince him. And now he had been shown.

It was to the words, nevertheless, that his mind returned – all the things that she had said on a previous occasion about attacking Lorillia ... With slow steps, he made his way back to the living room. Mistra was sitting on the sofa with her drink and his on a table in front of her. She looked at him searchingly as he came in, then shook her head.

'You still won't help me?' she asked.

'I can't.'

'Why not?'

He felt the need, curiously, to justify his attitude. And yet, he had no clear answer. He said finally, 'Why do you think you need me?'

She said simply, 'In the last war, bomber planes carried considerable crews, one to do this, one for that, a man for each task. I've rigged up relays that theoretically will enable me to do the job, but in practise I couldn't depend on it, not in the face of determined enemy fire.'

'You have to go down *that* low?'

Mistra nodded. 'We'll be in range, for a short time, of the most powerful anti-aircraft defense in the world. This ship of mine was not built for war. That's why they let me have it; so I was told today. They find it very easy to assume that no member of the group will seriously risk death.'

'And will you?'

'Allison, we've got to take the chance. There's no other way.'

Stephens groped for a suitable reply, found none, and finally said in an irritable tone, 'What I don't understand is, why the rush?'

'I received decisive news. The attack on the United States is set for October instead of next January.'

'Eight months away, and you're excited.' Stephens could almost feel the pressure lifting from inside him.

'You don't understand,' said Mistra. 'The bombs they'll use are still stored in groups. Now, they'll be dispersed within the next week or so to plane and submarine depots. Thereafter, only psychological pressure will be possible.'

She looked at him for a long minute, then said, 'You'll have to take my word for the attack and the danger.' She paused again; finally: 'Allison, this is your entry into the house.'

The offer was too unexpected for him to take it all at once. Stephens sat very still, his thoughts slowed as by shock. It did occur to him, vaguely, that he should have known that she would eventually make such a promise.

Actually, after all the information he had been given, there were only two things that the group could do with him. He must be taken into the Grand House – or killed! Mistra was now telling him that, for a price, she would try to get him in.

He stirred, conscious of that limitation. He wanted desperately to believe she could do it, but events and the fact that she herself was in danger, made her offer seem unreal. He said at last, drably, 'I doubt if you alone can open the Grand House for me.'

She said, 'I think I can.' Without looking at him, she went on, 'My dear, long life has its dark moments. There is the terror of thinking: What does it all mean? Where is it leading? Allison, I've played with tiny babies, and then *ninety* years later stood by untouched by time while one of those babies grown aged and withered, was laid forever into the ground. It's hard, I can tell you. Some of the others have adopted cynicism and callousness as a barrier between them and the cruelty of the life–death cycle. I was that way for a while. I lived for the moment. I had scores of lovers, one after another, abandoning each of them in turn at the first sign of aging.

'That phase passed, and for a time I lived almost like a nun. But that was a reaction. Slowly I began to develop a sounder philosophy of life – of *long* life. And strangely enough, that philosophy I was so slow in arriving at was, and is, based on simple things. The notion that what is healthy is good; the knowledge that the needs of the body and mind must balance; oh, and many other ideas that seem, in the telling, more trivial than they are. But there is one need which I have learned is more vital to a woman than any other, and it is one I have allowed to remain unsatisfied. Can you guess what it is?'

Stephens looked at her soberly, touched by the unusual warmth and earnestness in her low voice. Then the sudden awareness of what she meant brought him stirrings of excitement.

'You have never had a child. Is that it?'

Mistra nodded. 'The rule of the group is: No children. Several were born long ago, but were adopted out. It was remorselessly done, and I came to accept the attitude behind it as necessary.

'I no longer do. And so for ten years I've been looking for a suitable man to be the father of my child.'

She paused. She drew a deep breath. 'Allison, I suppose you've guessed that I want you to be that man.'

As she spoke, he felt her fingers gently touch his wrist. He hadn't noticed her reach toward him, and so the sudden contact was like a spark. The tingle of it went through his whole body. He caught her hand, held it tightly, then kissed it tenderly.

'But why me?' he said in a muffled tone.

'I know I'm being too intellectual, Allison, but it's only because there's no time to show you all I feel. And something must be done to save the Earth. I do love you – perhaps the first real love I've ever known.'

Her voice was soft. Stephens kissed her, still not quite believing. Her lips held to his with an intensity of response that left no doubt.

'Mistra,' he said, 'you're beautiful.'

She laughed in her rich contralto. 'And it's guaranteed forever. Don't forget that.'

He had forgotten. He tried to push away the thought that came. For a moment, he held her so tightly that she laughed and gasped. 'My dear man – air!'

Stephens took his arms from around her. He pulled away, and he said somberly, 'You speak of bringing a new life into the world. What about the thousands whose lives will be snuffed out when you make your attack?'

She looked at him, and shook her head wonderingly. 'I showed you the warning we'll issue.'

'They won't pay any attention to it, and you know it.'

She leaned toward him earnestly. 'Allison, the attack has to be made, regardless of casualties. You've got to help me.'

She went on quickly, 'Surely, you're not going to throw away your chance at the house – the chance for *our* love – I swear we'll give them every opportunity.'

'I notice you didn't mention – yourself?'

'There's no price on me.' She spoke simply. 'Only love can buy love. And that comes later.'

Just for a moment that caught him again; then silently, he shook his head. At last he said, 'I'm sorry, my dear, I'd give almost anything—' He stopped; he spread his hands helplessly.

'But you don't have to give anything.'

Stephens did not answer immediately, but his mind was set. If he took this step, he would no longer be a free agent, emotionally. He saw with a sharp awareness of his own feelings, that he could become pretty completely wrapped up in this woman. And then he wouldn't want to extricate himself. Here was the turning point. He must go back or go forward. Even to give love, he had to be true to his beliefs.

He felt no criticism. She believed in her purpose. This problem was entirely within his own being. There would be thousands of people in the factories that she wanted to bomb. They would be there despite any warning, and he simply could not help endanger them. He explained his feelings haltingly, for he felt like a fool; almost as if he lacked manhood.

But there was no doubt in his own mind. One woman and one man could not wage war against a nation. When he had finished his explanation, Mistra nodded thoughtfully, and said, 'I'll take you back to Almirante as soon as it gets dark.'

14

The night was dark and, except for the steady ocean breeze, the cemetery was silent. When Tannahill was an hour overdue, Mistra stirred in the seat beside him, and said softly:

'Perhaps the police waylaid him.'

Stephens said nothing, but he realized it was not impossible. In ordering Tannahill's arrest within an hour of returning to his office, Howland had taken a step from which there was no turning back. It could easily include road blocks.

Half an hour later – just before midnight – Mistra spoke again: 'Perhaps if I remained here, and you went somewhere and phoned the police to see if they had him —'

'Not yet. A lot of things could have delayed him.'

For a while there was silence again. He had suggested that the cemetery be the meeting place because it was a rendezvous with which both he and Tannahill were familiar.

Stephens went on finally, 'I've been doing a lot of thinking about your group. Have there been many quarrels among you in the past?'

'Not since we brought the mind-reader in two hundred years ago.'

'I intended to ask you why there was only one. I thought mind-reading might be a product of long life.'

'No.' Her reply was prompt. 'One of the members ran into a family in Europe who had a remarkable ability in that direction. So for two generations we tried an inbreeding experiment. We finally selected a grandchild.'

'You did this' – he hesitated – 'unanimously?'

He was aware of her turning and looking at him. 'What are you getting at?' she asked.

'I don't know.'

That was true. He was trying to fit together things that had so far not been explained. Why had he been shown the underground cave, and who was the man who had shown it to him? ... Mistra's motive in seeking his aid seemed clear enough. And she had evidently disarmed the mind-reader by the simple process of openly opposing the plan that the group had for leaving Earth.

Offhand, it was improbable that anyone could withhold a secret from a mind-reader for any length of time. It would mean keeping back certain thoughts only, and letting others come through; a problem in self-discipline that almost defied possibility. It seemed to suggest that the murders had been done by an outsider.

And yet, he himself had proved that a vital thought could be kept from the woman telepathist. In failing to notice that he had secured important information from the Mexican Import Company, she had revealed a weakness that someone in the group could have discovered previously. Stephens visualized the individual remaining away from the mind-reader as much as possible. And it was well to remember that the murder plan might have been conceived within the last year. The rebellion of Mistra had occupied but a moment in the history of the group.

Stephens said slowly, 'Did anyone oppose bringing in the mind-reader when the subject was first broached?'

'Yes' – her tone was slightly ironic – 'everyone except the person who had discovered the telepath.'

'Who was that?'

'Tannahill.'

'In view of his control of the house, I suppose he inevitably had his way.'

Mistra said seriously, 'He had the most important reason, of course. He suspected that there was dissatisfaction with his leadership, and he wanted incipient plotters to realize there was no hope.'

Stephens nodded. 'Who held out the longest?'

'It didn't work quite like that. You must understand that most of us are conservatives. We'd like to have the house set up as a sort of foundation with all of us acting as a board of directors. But, failing that, we would under normal circumstances prefer to let it remain in the control of Tannahill. Much as we dislike him, we *know* what our position is with him. Another owner would be an unknown quantity. So you see it wasn't very hard for us to be persuaded that a mind-reader might have a stabilizing effect. We simply asked recalcitrants what they were concealing, and when the matter finally came to a vote there was surprising unanimity. Well, not too surprising.' She laughed a little grimly.

Stephens said, 'Were there any previous attempts to take control of the house away from Tannahill? Before your attempt, I mean.'

'The owner before him – I suppose that could be called an attempt.'

'You're referring to the mysterious chief who occupied the house when Tanequila first arrived. Did he succeed? Did he get back in, I mean?'

'Yes, he did, and a good many of us went back with him.'

'You were among them?' It was the second surprise. 'You – preceded Tannahill?'

She was patient. 'Allison, you don't seem to be able to grasp how much time has gone by. I was in a ship where the passengers had to defend themselves against an uprising of the crew and the slave oarsmen. The passengers won, but we ran into a storm, and no one knew how to navigate. We touched land several times, once I think, equatorial Africa, then – I'm guessing – South America; and finally, completely lost though still intent on getting to our destination, we were swept around Cape Horn.'

'But why were you aboard that ship? Where were you going?' Stephens waited with fascinated interest.

She hesitated momentarily, then : 'I was at that time the

daughter of a Roman official in Britain.'

Stephens swallowed, and then asked, 'What year was that?'

'About A.D. 300.'

'The house is *that* old?'

'Immensely older than that. When we came ashore all the men in our party were killed by the owners. But they had been there for centuries.'

'But who built it?' Blankly.

'That's what we'd like to know,' she said grimly. 'We even thought it might be you. Remember?'

Stephens paused, and then took the plunge. 'Mistra, was Peeley the great chief before Tanequila came on the scene?'

'Yes.'

'How long has he been in the group?'

Silence.

'Mistra!'

'I'm thinking,' she said softly, 'Wait.'

'How good is your memory?'

'Perfect. But – *ssshh.*' More silence. At last, sighing, she spoke: 'Peeley was active in the experiments that led to our selection of a mind-reader. He was one of the first to join Tannahill in urging the presence of such a person. I think you're off the track, my dear.'

'Unless,' Stephens pointed out, 'he had discovered a method of concealing his thoughts.'

Mistra hesitated again, then: 'He's not in a position to do anything.'

'He's the attorney for the estate.'

Her voice was firmer. 'That's important but not decisive. We were so careful. I can't go into the details, but a separate office in Almirante under an outsider was one of the safeguards. Howland, you, others before both of you.'

'Why was Howland separated from the position?'

'He happened to notice that the signature on a document a hundred years ago was the same as on a recent one.'

Stephens laughed ironically. 'So he was replaced by a man who has now been told everything.'

'By me,' said Mistra. 'Nobody ever said that the group approved of it.' She broke off, 'Allison, it's one o'clock. And if you don't go and phone, I will. I really don't fancy sitting in a graveyard all night.'

Reluctantly, Stephens climbed out of the car. 'I suppose you're right,' he said. He looked at her shadowed figure behind the steering wheel. 'I'll go first to a drug store about two blocks from here. If they're closed, I'll go farther, if necessary all the way downtown.'

It seemed to him that Mistra nodded, but she said nothing. He leaned over and kissed her. At first her lips were only passive, then abruptly she put her arms up around his head. Stephens drew back presently, and said in a shaky tone, 'It might be advisable for you to get out of the car and wait in the shadows. That way you can watch anybody who approaches.'

Mistra answered that. 'Don't worry about me,' she said. 'I've got a gun.' Metal glinted in her hand. She spoke softly. 'Remember that saving the Earth is more important than anything – including us.'

Stephens walked swiftly along the road toward the gate. At the gate itself, he paused for a survey of the street opposite the cemetery. But his eyes saw no movement or sign of life.

He hurried across the road into the shadows of the trees that lined the street. The first drug store, as he had suspected, was closed. So was the second one. It was ten minutes to two when he entered an all-night cafe in the downtown business section and made his call to the police. The reply was terse but to the point. 'Arthur Tannahill has not yet been arrested.'

With a feeling of urgency he walked the two blocks to the nearest taxi stand. And then it was another two blocks to the cemetery gate from where he paid off the cabman. He jogged most of the way. The stamp of his shoes on the hard road merely transformed his impatience into sound. He slowed finally, puzzled.

He said softly to himself. 'The car was on this side of the

Tannahill plot.'

He walked a little farther, and then stopped. Dark as it was, he could see the grill-like fence of the Tannahill section. It was several feet behind him to the right. He stood very still. The road ahead of him and behind him was deserted. Mistra might have driven the Cadillac under the trees somewhere, but it seemed doubtful.

'Mistra!' he called. 'Oh, Mistra!'

No answer. And no sound but the heavy pounding of his heart. With a grim but hopeless patience, he set about searching the entire area. In fifteen minutes he was convinced.

Mistra and her car were no longer in the graveyard, nor was there any sign of Tannahill.

Stephens headed pessimistically for her apartment in a taxicab, and made certain she was not there. Nor was she at his own home. From there he called the Grand House, but there was no answer. Dismissing the cab, he got his car from the garage and drove back downtown. It was a few minutes of half past three in the morning as he approached the Palms Building.

A single light burned inside the lobby in front of the elevator shaft, but the doors were locked. That did not mean anything. Peeley had keys – and was, in fact, the only other man except for himself and the janitor who did have them legally.

Stephens slipped the key into the lock, then drew back, indecisive. Exactly what did he plan to do? He had his gun, which would take care of an emergency. But did he actually want Peeley to know that he had been identified?

The answer to that was no. But if Mistra was being held a prisoner —

Very softly, Stephens let himself into the building. He headed for the rear, and climbed the back stairs to the third floor. The office of the Mexican Import Company was dark. He listened at the door for several minutes, then moved slowly down the stairway to the sub-basement.

It took several minutes of tugging at the false wall to

force it open and enter the cavern beyond. Stephens found the lamp where he had left it, shut the secret door behind him, and stared hesitantly into the dimness ahead. There was no alternative. The cave was the only place left to look before he started on the drawn-out process of checking, one by one, the homes of the people he had identified as members of the group.

Shrugging, he began to move forward. The tunnel widened gradually on a downward slope, then leveled off. Since it was about a third of a mile to the bottom of the mountain atop which the Grand House stood, Stephens walked rapidly. After twenty minutes by his watch he reached the second tunnel where it branched off from the one he was in. Stephens turned along it without hesitation. As he came to the long wall of metal, he saw that a great section of it had lifted out of sight, and that beyond was a metal corridor.

He drew back hastily and clicked off his light. In the darkness, he waited with pounding heart. The minutes slipped by, and there was no sound.

He edged forward until he was at the door. He pressed flat against the door jamb, and peered inside. He could see a faint radiance, as if he were looking at a dull reflection of a very dim light.

He couldn't wait. Mistra might be in danger. Stephens turned on his light, and, Nambu in hand, went in.

He found himself in a broad, gleaming corridor that seemed to be lined with translucent glass. He paused several times to examine the material, but there were no openings that he could find. The 'glass' appeared to be unbroken.

He came to a large, domed chamber; and now he saw where the reflected light had come from. In one corner, almost hidden by rank on rank of shimmering glass, was a globe that glowed with a faint greenish radiance.

Stephens looked around him wonderingly. He had a sense of sounds just beyond the threshold of his reception. There was a vague, all-pervading vibration as if hidden machinery were pulsing and reacting perhaps to his presence. The whole effect was eerie and unnatural.

He could see that other corridors led off from the central room, but he did not immediately explore them. Instead, very carefully he approached the globe. It flickered with tiny light changes. The glow did not remain the same for more than a moment or so. Stephens was within five feet of the first glass barrier when, suddenly, a two foot square area of the globe facing him changed to a cream color, then turned white.

As he waited tensely, a picture took form. It showed a round, bright ball against a black background, with many dots of light visible in the darkness.

The bright ball grew rapidly larger, and presently Stephens saw that it had markings on it. He traced the familiar lines of North and South America, and the outjut of the Spanish peninsula.

Earth! He was being shown a scene from a spaceship approaching from outer space.

The planet quickly filled the picture area, and still it grew. Stephens saw the extended arm of lower California, then that became too vast for the screen's capacity.

For the first time he realized that the machine was coming down at least partly out of control. He had a glimpse of ocean, a brief view of a mountainous land; and then – crash!

It was all the more startling because it was so silent. One minute, the ship was plunging toward the side of a mountain; the next there was darkness.

Stephens thought almost blankly: 'Why, of course. This ship must have crashed here thousands of years ago. But who was in it?'

He saw that another picture was forming on the surface of the pulsating globe —

For two hours, Stephens watched. Entire series of the pictures were repeated several times, apparently for emphasis. Each time, new scenes were interpolated for clarification of otherwise obscure sequences. Gradually, a coherent, intelligible story emerged.

At an indeterminate time in the past, a robot-controlled spaceship, thrown far off course by a damaging accident, had crashed into the side of a cliff. The impact had precipitated a landslide, and the ship was buried under more than a hundred feet of soil and rock.

The robot survived the crash; and, since it was able to read minds as well as broadcast its own thoughts, it presently established contact with a small group of savages. It found that their minds were dominated by superstition, and implanted in them the irrational notion that they should dig a hole and open the way to the entrance of the ship.

But they were unable to repair the vessel, or to comprehend what was wanted. The robot projected into their minds the command that they construct a temple, each stone of which must first be brought into the ship for special treatment.

To impress the savages, the treatment was made a process of sparks and lightning flashes. The real treatment consisted of bombardment of the material by sub-atomic particles available in quantity only from very heavy and very rare, artificial elements. And the reason was to prolong the lives of those who might help the robot by repairing the ship.

Of that first group of primitives who lived long, all but one were eventually killed by violent means. Among the novitiates who replaced the dead, Stephens was startled to see a tall, light-skinned man who resembled, and therefore undoubtedly was, Walter Peeley.

It was Peeley and the smaller man – the only survivor of the first group – whose minds awakened to the possibility that the ship was not a god. The robot-brain welcomed them, and secretly began to give them a scientific education. They learned, among other things, which part of the robot was the thought receiver and which the thought sender.

It was the robot that discovered that newer priests of the temple were receiving some of the thoughts it was transmitting. As a protection from the resulting suspicion, it showed its two adherents how to adjust the thought sender, so that its range would be limited to the ship.

They shut it off completely.

It was a sudden impulse. The hostility behind it came out of some depth of hate and fear in the mind of the smaller man.

Both men were instantly in a state of terror. Using the weapons they had found in its storeroom, they destroyed the sensitive sender.

In automatic defense, the robot released a gas into the interior. Coughing, their bodies contorted by pain, the two fled. The door shut behind them.

They were never admitted again. With the passage of time, they analyzed what had happened, and, with the scientific knowledge they had, guessed a great deal more. They murdered all the rest of the second group, filled in the open pit, and had the caves dug. They planned to get aboard the vessel again, and seize its cargo.

The robot wanted only to have the ship repaired, so that it could resume its journey. It was vaguely aware that many plans were afoot, and realized finally it would have to take some risks.

One day, the two men came into the cave with drilling equipment. But the metal walls of the ship were impregnable to the diamond-hard cutting tools. During this visit, the robot realized that the smaller man was urging action against the others of the group, but that Peeley seemed to be resisting.

The atomic-war crisis stimulated the smaller man to a final, decisive plan. Just what his scheme was, the robot could not determine. The plotter remained warily at a distance, out of thought reach.

He shot Tannahill, intending to kill, intending that Peeley, as attorney for the estate, would control disposal of the property. His boundless ambition included domination of the world ... But his was a face which Stephens had never seen. If he were still around, he must be wearing a mask.

When the pictures finally ceased, Stephens spent a few minutes walking through the 'hold' examining the ship's cargo. According to the films – he assumed it was a film record he had been shown – the long, shielded shelves were loaded with tiny, gleaming capsules, each one of which contained a small amount of an artificial element in pure form.

They were elements unknown on Earth, elements so far beyond Uranium on the periodic table that, if they had ever existed in nature, it must have been for a mere moment in the history of the universe.

Stephens had no idea what he would do with them. They seemed to have no value in the present situation. It was even doubtful if he could find a buyer ... unless he sold them to the group ...

It was a quarter of six when Stephens wearily re-entered the sub-basement of the Palms Building, and started up the steps. One thing was beginning to worry him: There was no indication of who Peeley's murderous companion might be.

It seemed vital that he be identified and exposed to the group.

Stephens reached the main floor of the Palms Building, stood for a moment in the alcove behind the elevator, and started up toward his office. As he came to the halfway landing, and turned to climb the rest of the way, he saw a man's legs move into view. Stephens' hand flashed to his pocket. His fingers poised on the gun; and then slowly he brought his hand out again, empty.

'Well,' he said, 'Bill Riggs.'

15

In Stephens' office, Riggs began, 'Well, Mr. Stephens, I've got the dope on Newton Tannahill's burial. The undertaker was the Almirante Mortuary, then owned by a Norman Moxley, who bought the place a few months before the funeral and sold out immediately afterward.'

He paused; and Stephens nodded. This was drab information, compared to the heady stuff he had learned on the ship. And yet it was not less vital. Knowing the overall back history gave him a sharper picture of the situation; perhaps it even strengthened his ultimate bargaining position. But actually here in Almirante he was still concerned with the charge against Tannahill.

He doubted that Moxley had left town. A mask had been donned and then discarded. It might be possible to find out what important citizens had been 'out' of the city during the period of Moxley's stay, and so by a process of elimination identify the member of the gang who played the role. But it would not be possible to *prove* that such a masquerade had, in fact, taken place.

He realized that a comment was expected. He said aloud, 'That sounds bad. The district attorney could use that against Mr. Tannahill.'

'Well, it isn't good,' Riggs admitted, 'and the dope I got on the doctor is on the same lines. His name is Doctor Jaime de las Cienegas. He graduated from UCLA fifteen years ago, but never practiced till he settled in Almirante in December of last year. He sold his practice for a hundred dollars on May fifteenth last, and left town the next day. A slippery son of a gun, if you ask me.'

Stephens was curious. 'Where did you get this information?'

'I started comparing the telephone book current at the time of the burial with the latest edition. Dr. de las Cienegas' name was in the former, and not in the latter, and the Almirante Mortuary is now called the Benson Brothers Funeral Parlor. I called on them and learned some of the stuff I told you, and I learned that when they had bought the place the escrow work had been done by the local branch of the Bank of America. It was from the manager of the bank that I found out how much Moxley had paid for the place.

'Both the Bensons and the bank manager describe Moxley as a tall Englishman, reserved, distinguished-looking, polite. And they had heard that he had a passion for gambling, but had no direct knowledge about that. They judged him to be about forty years old.'

'And what about the doctor?' Stephens asked, wondering how he could use the information against Peeley.

'I found out about him from the secretary of the local branch of the medical association. He was quite a friendly duck, I understand, rather sardonic in his outlook, but apparently well liked by the other doctors. His hobby was poisons. He had a terrific library on the subject, but since poisons didn't enter this case I didn't push that angle.'

He paused and looked questioningly at Stephens. His eyes were narrowed ever so slightly, and Stephens had the impression that the detective was watching his reactions closely, and that the man knew more than he was telling.

He was not so sure that poisons were not involved in the case. Certainly these people used drugs for specific purposes like producing amnesia. It could be something to go into, but later.

Now, he saw sharply that his side of this meeting had been suspiciously unrevealing, and that Riggs might legitimately speculate on why Allison Stephens was wandering around in the early morning hours. Some explanation was needed. Besides, it might be well to make the detective his confidant to some extent.

'Mr. Riggs,' he began, 'Mr. Tannahill and I had pretty well come to the conclusion that a large group was operating this affair, and that a great deal of money was involved. My own investigations seem to prove that the situation is very complex indeed.'

He described what Howland had said about Mistra's income, and mentioned again the letter that Tannahill had been compelled to sign. He did not describe Mistra as the source of his information, but gave it as his opinion that the members of the group were now financially dependent on the Tannahill estate. He told of the cave, but he gave a false account of having stumbled upon it.

He did not mention the ship, immortality, cults, masks, or how he had originally run into the group. He finished, 'Your problem and mine, Mr. Riggs, is very difficult. In one sense we should try to bring this group into the light of day, but would it do our employer any good? We must be careful and not make any more enemies for Mr. Tannahill than he already has. It's possible that we'll have to find the real murderer.'

Riggs nodded, and seemed lost in thought. 'This cave,' he said finally, 'do you think it has any bearing on the case?'

Stephens hesitated; then: 'I doubt it!' he lied.

'Then let's forget it.' Riggs went on, earnestly, 'I tell you, Mr. Stephens, these references to amnesia, secret caves, and gangs scare me. I think we'd be well advised not to bring stuff like that into the open.' He broke off, 'And now, I might as well be honest and admit I've been following you most of the day.'

'Following me!' echoed Stephens. His feeling of blankness yielded to anxiety. Swiftly, he went back in his mind over the events of the night. Except for the cave incident he had done nothing that Riggs couldn't know about and there was no sign that he knew anything about that. Relieved, Stephens said, 'That puzzles me.'

Riggs went on: 'How did I know you weren't in this thing against the guy that hired me? I figured I'd better check on you. It got a little monotonous in the graveyard, all four of us sitting around doing nothing.'

That pulled Stephens out of his calm. He half-rose from his chair, then slowly settled back again. 'Four?' he said at last.

'I don't know whether you're going to like this,' said Riggs, 'but he'd been waiting there for a couple of hours for you to go —'

'Who had?'

'Tannahill.' Riggs paused, then went on, 'I got the impression that he and the girl had talked to each other earlier. Anyway, when you finally left, he went over to her. He said something about making sure that she'd meant what she'd said. And she said, "Yes, I'll marry you".' Riggs paused. 'Then he got into the car, and they drove off to Las Vegas.'

He stopped; and his blue eyes were sympathetic, as he went on, 'I can see that hits you hard. Sorry!'

Stephens grew slowly aware that he was hunched up in his chair, and that his face muscles were taut, his teeth clenched, his eyes hurting. He swallowed half a dozen times in rapid succession, and each time it hurt his throat more. With an effort, he repressed his emotion, and said stiffly, 'What happened then?'

'You came back, and I followed you all over town. When you got to the Palms Building, you went in and locked the door after you. I spent two hours getting in through a third story window, and then we met in the corridor. That's the picture.'

Stephens nodded, and said finally, 'I think we'd both better get some sleep.'

There were innumerable things to do. Arrange for bail if needed. Details of defense. Preparation of legal papers. That would be his open activity. The rest concerned his preparations for approaching the group. He had to be in the strongest possible position.

As he bade Riggs good night, he was thinking that what Mistra had done followed inexorably from his refusal. Failing to obtain his help, she had taken a more determined step. He remembered her saying – her last words – that saving Earth was more important than their love.

She had Tannahill. She could threaten the group through him.

Wearily, Stephens stretched out on the cot in the rest room that led off from the clerical section of his office.

He had still not slept when Miss Chainer arrived at eight-thirty. He went down to the barbershop in the building next door, had a shave, and then went across the street for breakfast. He was heading back to his office, when he saw an assay office sign half a block away. It was not the first time he had noticed it, but he had never before thought of it in relation to himself.

Involuntarily, his fingers sought in his coat pocket for the bits of marble he had taken from the Grand House steps. He entered the shop and handed the chips to the man behind the counter. He asked, 'How soon can you give me an analysis of these?'

The assayer was a lean, oldish man who wore gold-rimmed glasses. He countered Stephens' question with one of his own : 'How soon do you want it?' He mumbled something about the holidays.

Stephens cut him off : 'Look, I'll pay you double if I can have it tomorrow morning.'

Briskly, the man gave him a receipt. 'About ten,' he said.

As Stephens emerged from the shop, a newsboy was shouting : 'Read all about the Lorillian attack!'

16

Stephens bought a paper with fingers that shook. The headline in full was: LORILLIA ACCUSES U.S. OF ATTACK.

Below that, in smaller caps, was: AMBASSADOR HANDS PROTEST NOTE TO STATE DEPARTMENT.

The story began: 'The United States Government categorically denied today that U.S. warplanes attacked factories and installations in Lorillia at noon (Lorillian time) today. Secretary of State Walter Blake has announced the government's rejection of the protest —'

Stephens' eyes were already skipping, seeking for information more substantial than protests and accusations. He came to a paragraph that read:

'Diplomatic observers were puzzled by the Lorillian accusation, few giving any credence to the account. However, from Antulla has come a report that inter-plane radio messages were picked up at the capital, in which Lorillian pilots reported to their bases that they were unable to continue pursuit of the enemy ships, which had apparently escaped by climbing out of their reach. From claims and counter-claims of various pilots, Antulla observers conclude that some damage was inflicted on the attackers, though there is no evidence that any was shot down —'

Stephens kept swallowing as he read the account. He pictured the scene, Mistra coming down through a veritable hell of guided missiles, anti-aircraft rockets, and high explosive shells. The newspaper account was evidence that she had persisted in the face of the heaviest fire. She had risked her immortal body – for what? For a world that would possibly never know that it had been in danger.

There seemed no doubt but that a number of ships had

participated in the attack, but that hardly mattered. The group had capitulated out of fear. Confronted with a deadly threat against Tannahill, alarmed by the possible complications, they had helped her carry out her plan.

It was a major change of policy. The Grand House would stay where it was. The group would remain on Earth. Unless the baffled and angry Lorillians forced issues there would be no war.

Just before noon, Stephens called the district attorney's office, and after a moment's delay got through to Howland, who said coldly, 'You realize that Mr. Tannahill's departure is evidence of guilt? This proves I was right to issue a warrant for his arrest, Stephens.'

Stephens, wary of recording devices, expressed astonishment at such a statement. 'After all,' he said very distinctly, 'a man who does not even know he is to be arrested can hardly be accused of running away.'

'Now, look here, Stephens —' Howland began.

'It is possible,' lied Stephens, 'that Mr. Tannahill has gone to San Francisco for New Year's Eve. He mentioned to me that he was anxious for a little excitement. As soon as I hear from him, I'll advise him of your action. Meanwhile, I am making application for bail to Judge Adams, and will ask for an early hearing.'

On the way back to his office after lunch, he turned in at the Downtown Bookstore. He said to the clerk, 'Have you anything on the subject of longevity?' The man said, 'Oh, you mean books on Geriatrics.'

Stephens supposed so, though it was a new word to him. He followed the man along a line of shelves, watched him examine a row of titles.

'Ah!' the clerk brought out a thin volume. ' "The Prolongation of Life" by the Russian, Bogomolets. He tells you to eat Bulgarian yogurt, which contains bacteria that destroy toxic bacteria in your intestines. I take it all the time myself; but it's too soon to tell if it's going to do the job.' He laughed.

The clerk went on, 'Now, over here we have the pam-

phlet, "Live Long and Like It", put out by the Public Affairs
Committee in New York. Their idea is, periodic physical
examinations. If anything is wrong anywhere, spare no ex-
pense till it's fixed up. You're as young as your oldest organ;
that's the idea. What's the good of having a forty-year-old
heart and a ninety-year-old liver?'

Stephens examined the pamphlet, and finally nodded his
acceptance of it. He said hesitantly, 'Anything on' – he
stumbled over the word – 'de-differentiation?'

He explained, and the clerk shook his head, but finally
said doubtfully, 'We've got a book that deals with chame-
leons – fascinating.'

Stephens bought that as well as the pamphlet and the
Bogomolets volume. He returned to his office, conscious for
the first time of how tremendous was the pressure that was
driving him.

Stephens sat down at his desk, and thought: In all
Almirante there was only one man who had enough legal
power – and some motivation – to take action against the
group: Frank Howland. Howland could arrest, appeal ad-
verse decisions to higher courts, command public attention,
and obtain search warrants. The problem would be to give
Howland enough information to stimulate him, but not
enough to enable him to guess the truth.

Frank Howland ... partner. Stephens laughed without
amusement, and thought: 'I'll call him tomorrow.'

He picked up the phone, dialed the airport, and chartered
a plane to take him to Los Angeles at midnight that night.

He went out and bought a spade and a pickaxe, and put
them in his car. Tonight he must check on the one aspect of
this affair of which he had no definite proof. These people
might be immortal, but he had only somebody's word for
that.

Back in his office, he took out his notebook, and wrote:
'Assuming all that I've learned is true, what remains to be
investigated?'

Plenty, but surprisingly little that he could approach
directly. The death of Jenkins and the Negro caretaker had

still to be explained, as well as who had written the note to Howland. Peeley's role as co-conspirator with the unidentified Indian remained obscure.

What was the plan the two were working on? Why had the smaller man secretly opposed the move away from Earth, to the extent of trying to murder Tannahill when the latter agreed to move the Grand House? And how did he hope to use Allison Stephens to force the robot brain to capitulate?

His own problem, Stephens decided finally, narrowed down to one overall question:

How could he use the information he had to trap the murderer, frustrate the group, and gain the Grand House for himself, Mistra – and the rest of the world?

He glanced at his watch. It was five to four. At least five hours to go before he could do anything decisive.

He visited the morgue which, in Almirante, was attached to a funeral parlor. He verified that Ford had died from a bullet wound; Jenkins had been stabbed. 'Funny thing about that knife wound,' said the attendant. 'You'd have thought he was killed by a red-hot knife. The wound was all blistered.'

Needle beam!

Stephens felt an icy thrill. He spent the rest of the afternoon and part of the evening checking the addresses he had gotten from the account book at the Mexican Import Company. The group of names that emerged represented a good part of the economic power of that part of the state.

More than ever, he felt the handicap of one ordinary man pitting himself against so much intrenched power.

He had dinner, and then shortly before nine drove home and put on an old pair of trousers, a heavy shirt, and a sweater. The night was cloud-filled, which made it easy to drive into the cemetery, and to the Tannahill plot. He sat for minutes, waiting for a sign that he had been seen. But the silence rivaled that of the night before. Grave opening was evidently not considered a sufficient hazard by the local police to take precautions against it.

Stephens climbed out of the car. His intention was to open two graves. The first one (Francisco Tanequila who had died in 1770) and the other to be selected at random. After an hour he was still sweating away in a shallow hole that he had cut into the first grave. He was appalled at the adobe-like hardness of the ground, and when another hour had passed, he began seriously to consider abandoning the project. The blackness of the night decided him to stay. The decision paid off as his shovel abruptly struck softer dirt. Less than half an hour after that, he brought up a piece of rotted wood, and shortly after that he penetrated into the coffin and unearthed the stones.

There were a dozen of them with a total weight of about a hundred and eighty pounds. Stephens made sure the coffin contained nothing else, then he filled in the grave, and sat down for a rest. He knew now that he would have to open a second grave.

He tested several by sinking his shovel into them. The softest dirt drew his shovel again, and soon he was digging forcefully. But he had only gone a foot when he struck something that resisted his thrust. The resistance was of such a curious nature that Stephens bent down with his flashlight, and clawed at the dirt with his fingers. Human clothing.

In a few minutes of careful scraping with his hands, he had the head uncovered. It was defaced beyond recognition. Stephens flinched as he studied it, but after a moment's thought he exposed one of the hands, and took his sun glasses out of their case. Carefully, he impressed the imprint of the forefinger on the inside of one of the lenses, and the thumb on the inside of the other. He returned the glasses to their case, and slipped the case into his pocket.

Very carefully, an emptiness in his stomach, Stephens covered the body and headed for home. It was after midnight, and he had still to go to the airport. He drove home without incident, called the airport, and asked that the pilot he had hired wait for him. Then he bathed and dressed.

About one o'clock the plane took off, and landed half an

hour later at a remote southern appendage of Western Avenue. A taxi took him to the Sunset Strip, where Peeley had his law office in a Spanish-type court. The place was in darkness, the whole series of shops and offices untenanted at this hour of the night.

He was prepared to break in, but one of the keys from Mistra's purse fitted; and it was a simple matter then of finding the letter that Tannahill had signed, authorizing Peeley to 'continue' the payments the estate had been making to 'members of the Pan-American Club'.

Stephens slept most of the way back to Almirante, and went to bed immediately when he got home.

He was downtown again by noon.

He had examined his sun glasses during the night, and the fingerprints of the dead man had seemed clear. Now, in the light of day, he took them out again; and there was no doubt about it. Each lens had an unblurred print on it.

Stephens studied them, finally took out his handkerchief and partly removed the mark of the forefinger. For his purposes, it was a little pat to have both prints so good. The precaution taken, he headed for the police station, and gave the glasses to the officer in charge of the fingerprint bureau. He explained:

'A few days ago I reported that vandals had cut my phone wires. This morning I found these glasses lying in the grass nearby. I thought it might be worth finding out if you could photograph the prints and have them checked.'

The bespectacled lieutenant examined the glasses with interest. 'Sure,' he said, 'we'll get 'em. We'll call you, Mr. Stephens.'

Stephens turned to go, then slowly faced the man again. The crises he was forcing might not wait on a slow investigation. He asked, 'I have a vague notion that you'll have to check them either with Washington or the driver's license division at Sacramento. How long will that take?'

The officer said casually, 'If we don't have a record here, it'll take a week maybe.'

Stephens gloomily guessed two weeks, hesitated once

more, then said, 'I also understand that you can wire.'

'For a vandal?' the man was astounded.

Stephens said, 'I'm curious, and besides, I'm not too ready to dismiss the incident as unimportant. So I'll pay the expenses of a wire check-up. How about getting me an authorization form to sign?'

Stephens stopped in next at the assay office. The old man came out of the rear, blinking. 'You're a fine one,' he said. 'Offer extra money for a job by ten, then don't come in.'

'I'll still pay the extra,' said Stephens.

The other seemed relieved. He began. 'Chemically, there was nothing unusual about the sample. It was ordinary calcium carbonate in the form of marble.'

'Damn!' said Stephens.

'Not so fast.' The old man was grinning. 'I'm not finished.' Stephens waited.

'Lately, with so much prospecting for pitchblende going on, we've included tests with the electroscope as part of our routine, and surprisingly, your stuff was radioactive.'

He stared at Stephens triumphantly, and repeated: 'Radioactive ... Very slight. I was unable to recover any residue. And, when separated, the calcium, the carbon, and the oxygen were not in themselves radioactive. Very interesting. If it leads to anything, how about sending the business our way?'

'If you'll keep quiet about it for now,' said Stephens.

'What do you think I've been doing?' was the retort.

Outside again, he thought: Radioactivity. It explained everything and it explained nothing. It was a facet of nature that man had by no means thoroughly explored.

He had a sudden vision of men living in houses made radioactive in exactly the right fashion and so immortalizing themselves.

He wondered if the robot was limited in the extent of its operations? Or could the process be enlarged to include more than a privileged few; or even duplicated perhaps to include all mankind?

17

He drove to the editorial offices of the *Almirante Herald*. But Carewell, its publisher, was 'out of town'. He phoned Judge Porter, Judge Adams, and a dozen others of the group: 'Gone for the holidays' 'Out of town' 'Expected back tomorrow'.

Stephens left a message each time, asking to be called at any time, day or night, whenever the absentee returned.

He ate lunch, then went to his office, and sat at his desk thinking over what he had done. He was committed. He could not undo the phone calls he had made. The group members, returning home, would find his message. When they checked with each other, it would become clear that he knew who they were.

From their point of view, he would seem an intruder – a man who knew too much.

He had to make his position stronger. He had to have them where *he* could make an attack on them if necessary.

He was still considering how he might do so, and through whom, when Miss Chainer buzzed him. 'Oh, Mr. Stephens, Mr. Howland is calling you.'

Stephens felt a peculiar thrill. Why, of course, he thought, almost breathlessly, that's *one* way.

It would be a facet only, but not unimportant. The police might be very useful indeed in a crisis.

Howland's voice said, a moment later, 'I want you to come to my office some time this afternoon. Can you make it?'

'How about right now?' said Stephens.

'Fine.'

He hung up. And it was only slowly that his tension let

go. It struck him then that he had been so intent on the vital things he had to say to Howland that it hadn't occurred to him to wonder what Howland wanted to say to him.

He sighed, because the plunge was taken. And there was no turning back. Once more, he called to see if either the publishers or the judges were available. They weren't.

Stephens left his name.

He drove to the courthouse, and was immediately admitted to the inner sanctum. Howland strode from behind his desk as Stephens entered, and offered his hand. Then: 'Sit down!'

Stephens sat.

Howland returned to his own chair, and said slowly: 'Stephens, we finally located beyond question the fingerprints of Newton Tannahill. They do not match those of his nephew, Arthur. Accordingly, I've made a grave mistake in ordering Tannahill's arrest.'

He paused, and seemed to be studying Stephens' face for a reaction. Stephens with difficulty maintained a poker expression. He said coolly, 'I told you you were acting hastily.'

Howland's teeth clamped hard together. 'Damn it,' he said, 'why the hell weren't there any prints earlier?' He calmed; then: 'I need your help.'

Stephens scarcely heard. The first blank feeling in his mind gave way to a great wonder. The group had actually solved the problem of altering fingerprints. He could only guess at the method but it must be part of the de-differentiation process. As the cells returned to their youth, the decisive change could be made. It was hard to believe that there could be any other satisfactory explanation, unless he was prepared at this late date to dismiss the immortality aspect of the affair as a hoax. He realized, rather grimly, that he was not prepared to do so.

He brought his mind back to what Howland had said, and considered the bearing it might have on what he himself had to say to Howland. He decided that it did not change the situation appreciably.

Howland leaned forward. 'Stephens,' he said, 'I'm prepared to forget the past. It's over; and I've got my wits
about me again. Here's the problem: I'll be ruined if I
simply withdraw the charge. If you can suggest a way out,
we'll do business.'

Stephens had to fight a tension that almost knotted his
stomach muscles. Because here was the opportunity he had
wanted. He said, 'I'll show you exactly how we can clear
Mr. Tannahill.'

'Go on!' said Howland softly.

Coolly, pausing only for breath, Stephens described the
whipping of Mistra, but gave no indication of who the
people were that had whipped her. He named no names,
made no mention of spaceships, the cave, immortality, or
the robot-ship under the mountain. Instead, he concentrated
on the notion that a number of people belonging to a cult
were apparently obtaining money from the Tannahill
estate. And that that alone explained the caretaker's murder
and all subsequent events.

When he finally left the district attorney's office, it
seemed to Stephens that he had taken another big step into
darkness.

He drove up to the Grand House. As he rounded the
clump of trees and came within sight of that noble tier of
steps, he half-expected to see signs of life around the estate.

He rang the doorbell for several minutes, without an
answer. He could have let himself in with one of Mistra's
keys, but instead he walked to the edge of the terrace,
jumped to the grass below, and walked around to the back.

The house looked dark and uneven as seen from the rear,
silhouetted against the light blue heaven and the dark blue
sparkling sea. The silence of isolation lay upon the structure, and the weight of unthinkable age was heavy over all
the land as well as the building.

The house stood in the sun. And there seemed little question that, to it, murder was an old story, violence common
and intrigue as natural as the life and death cycles it had

been built to circumvent. The house that was old was as full of secrets as of years, its bland walls hiding a bloody history ...

All the out-buildings were well back from the house, being separated from it by a series of flower gardens and two lines of high shrubs. Trees had been planted skilfully beside each building to shield its uglier aspects from the view of those who dwelt in the house.

He came to the east slope of the hill. A shallow valley spread below him, and in the distance among trees he could see a green-roofed farmhouse. Then more hills rolling away to the horizon. Stephens followed the crest of the hill to where the road came down to a cliff's edge – the same road and the same cliff toward which Mistra had driven her car.

By the time he returned to the nearest out-building, he had his first overall picture of the Grand House and its environs. The sun was low in the western sky, and the water an endless, glittering spectacle. Stephens had little interest in breaking through the padlocks that barred the doors of the nine rear buildings. He guessed that they contained nothing of significance. It was the house that mattered.

He let himself into the front door of the Grand House, and explored each of the dozen rooms. There were eight bedrooms, a spacious library, a dining room, the living room, and an enormous kitchen. Every room had French doors leading onto a closed patio.

He stood finally in the hall, and studied the structural design of the interior of the building. He saw that there had originally been three principal archways, which had been skilfully reconstructed, two rooms to each section.

It was growing dark as Stephens started down the hill. He was vaguely depressed. He had still to find a clue to the identity of the Indian who was the sole survivor of the first men who had lived in the house.

He had dinner in town, and drove home. He put his car away, and he was heading toward the house when a rope looped out from behind a bush, and dropped neatly over his shoulders. The noose drew tight around his elbows, and simultaneously he was jerked off his feet.

The blow of the fall stunned him, and he was unable to resist as the rope was wound around him and a gag was stuffed into his mouth.

18

'All right, Stephens, get up and come along!'

Stephens! The use of his name ended the vague hope that this was merely a gang of night marauders. Stephens climbed to his feet, and staggered as strong hands gripped his topcoat, and tore it halfway down his back – snatched at his suit coat and simultaneously ripped that and his shirt. Half naked, he was jerked against the trunk of a tree. The rope was wound around the trunk.

It was only seconds after that that there was a thin, whistling sound. And a whip bit into his bare shoulders.

Stephens gasped. It was as if a knife had slashed across his back. The second lash took his breath away, and brought the shrinking fear that the whip would tear his face and eyes. Clenching his teeth, he pressed his head against the tree bole. By God, he thought, they'd pay for this!

It held him, that thought, that fury, as the whip reached for him vindictively. The pain lost its terrible sharpness and became a numb sensation. His knees began to sag, and a mist coated his brain. Just when the whipping ceased, he had no clear idea, but suddenly a voice said grimly:

'We could have killed you. As it is, you have now received a warning. If you ever again concern yourself with our affairs for any reason, we'll mark you for life. We'll blind you. We'll cut your pretty face to ribbons.'

They must have gone away, for there was silence while he sagged against the tree. His strength came back slowly, and the first light was brightening the eastern sky when he realized that his legs were able to support him again. He grew aware that the loose end of the rope was merely tucked into one of the coils. He worked his arm around to the side of the tree. And tugged the rope free.

He collapsed on the grass, and lay breathing heavily. At last he started for the house. Stephens unlocked the door, staggered into the living room, and lay down on the sofa.

After a while he went into his bedroom, and stripped, and rubbed a soothing salve over the broken flesh. He cleansed and dressed it, then made some coffee. By the time he had finished his first cup, his anger had subsided, and he was feeling a lot better.

He spent the morning and part of the afternoon lying down. His courage returned slowly, and it seemed clear to him that the group didn't realize how much he knew. It was hard to believe that otherwise they would seriously expect him to give up.

The stakes were beyond any resistance they might offer. An immortal group, living secretly in a land of mortal men, had been briefly forced into the open by the action of one or more of their members and by an imminent atomic war. Now, unaware of the schemes of the mysterious Indian, they were trying to close ranks. If they succeeded, the mists would begin to come down, vagueness settle over events. If they succeeded, all too soon in the natural course of events, Allison Stephens would go down into the shadows with the murdered John Ford and William Jenkins. Become another name on the lists of the dead of some day not too far distant. A few years, a few decades, a moment in eternity. Entirely apart from his blurred plan to make longevity available to all humanity, his personal need was in itself great enough to force him to go on regardless of danger.

About half past two, Stephens was so far recovered that he got up, shaved and dressed, and ate lunch out of the refrigerator. Then he dialed the Grand House. After several rings, the receiver at the other end clicked, and a woman's voice said, 'This is the housekeeper. Who is calling, please?'

It was the voice of *Gico Aine*! The group was back all right.

Stephens identified himself, waited as she apparently turned away from the phone, and then she said coolly: 'Mr. Tannahill asks me to tell you that he has said all that he cares to say in the letter he sent to your office.'

'Letter?' said Stephens, puzzled.

He caught himself. 'Is Miss Lanett there?'

'Miss Lanett is also not available for you.'

Click!

Stephens slowly replaced the receiver; then he drove down to the office. As he came in, Miss Chainer said:

'There's a registered, special delivery letter on your desk. It's marked "personal", so I didn't open it.'

'Thank you!' said Stephens automatically.

He read the letter with pursed lips:

Dear Mr. Stephens:

    This is to notify you that your contract with the estate is terminated as of now. You will please mail your keys to the Grand House, and walk out of the office within the hour. Adequate separation compensation will be made to you in due course.

        Yours truly,

        Arthur Tannahill.

Stephens folded the letter, and put it in his breast pocket. He was keyed up, he realized, but not depressed.

The group was unloading him. There would be other pressures. Even the reference to 'compensation in due course' was a tactical move. Perhaps, if he agreed to leave Almirante his severance pay might be large indeed.

He phoned Riggs' hotel, and this time got through almost immediately. Riggs said, 'I'm sorry, Mr. Stephens. Reason I didn't call you was that I received a letter from Mr. Tannahill saying you were no longer connected with the case, and to have nothing to do with you.'

'You received a letter *only*? No personal contact?'

'No.'

'Not even a phone call?'

'What are you getting at?' Riggs sounded vaguely alarmed.

'Look, Bill' – seriously – 'I have every reason to believe that Mr. Tannahill is a prisoner. Have you received your walking papers?'

'Well – the letter said I wouldn't be needed any more, and that I was to put in my bill— Hell, you mean we're being had? I was packing.'

'Better unpack – unless you want to get out of the deal.'

'I'm staying right here. Where'll we meet?'

'No place. I'm going to force a showdown with some pretty dangerous people, and I need your help in a big way...'

He phoned the newspapers. Neither Carewell nor Grant were in – at least, so he was told. In each case he talked instead to the managing editor. He told both editors: 'Impress upon your publisher that a big story is going to break tonight. He knows where it will be. He's the only press representative who will be invited, and he's got to come personally. Tell him everyone in the group must be there.'

Next, he called Judges Porter and Adams and, unable to get through to the men, talked to their secretaries. Those were the only calls he made to members of the group. The rest would have to learn by grapevine and turn up without invitation.

Stephens was pretty sure they would be there. The group and the murderer. The egomaniac and his next victims. The man who aspired to dominate an entire planet and those who stood in his way.

That had to be the answer. The man was taking too many risks. At any moment the other members of the group might discover that somebody among them was doing something secretively. And surely, surely, that must be the one unforgivable crime.

He had to kill them to save himself.

Thought of killing reminded Stephens of the dead man in

the Tannahill burial plot. He phoned the police, and learned that the fingerprint identification had not yet come through. He groaned, as he hung up. He was forcing a showdown for this very night, and he still didn't have that vital piece of information.

Restlessly, he took out a notepad, and wrote: *The dead man is either not connected with this affair, or he is. I've got to assume that he is.*

He hesitated, then scrawled: *He's not somebody I know. He is somebody I know.*

Stephens stared gloomily at the sheet. It was straining logic to assume the latter possibility. And yet, his analysis ended immediately if he didn't assume it. He wrote: *Assume I know him. Who is he?*

After a moment's thought, he wrote down a heading: *Physical characteristics of dead body: About my build. Who do I know in this affair that's my size? ... Walter Peeley.*

He paused there. For the improbable identification was flashing signals in his mind. Swiftly, he picked out the logical highlights of the chain of reasoning: Peeley had been missing for a week; Jenkins had seen him on the night of Mistra's whipping, but despite many attempts to locate him, he had not been seen after that date.

The robot brain had indicated that Peeley had long opposed his companion's more violent schemes. It seemed plausible that now that the crisis was here, the man had finally murdered his careful colleague – this despite the precautions that Peeley (according to the robot) had secretly taken against the other.

More strongly than ever, it emphasized that this was the decisive hour. Equally convincing was the fact that the murderer did not seem to be worried that Allison Stephens would tell the group about the ship. And yet he had held that information back for more than a thousand years.

Either he didn't care any more or – what was far more likely – he was utterly confident of success.

Stephens was still thinking about it a moment later when his door opened. Miss Chainer came in, swallowed, and then gulped: 'There's a Miss Lanett to see you.'

As the vision that was Miss Lanett entered, Miss Chainer seemed to fade away like a wisp of autumn-brown hay. The door closed, and Stephens stared at Mistra with bright eyes.

His excitement ended almost immediately. For she returned his gaze coolly, then walked over to a chair. 'May I sit?' she asked.

Stephens studied her somberly. He guessed that he was about to receive another rebuff. He said finally, 'I see you won your point in your attack on Lorillia.'

She nodded. 'Did it shock you?'

He shook his head. 'I still could not have participated in it, but since you believed that you were right —' He broke off. 'Did you marry Tannahill?'

For a long time, she studied him. 'Where did you get that notion?' she asked at length.

Stephens had no intention of betraying Riggs, now that the detective was to play so prominent a role in the showdown later in the evening. He said, 'It was the logical solution. Marry Tannahill. And automatically own half his property under California law.'

There was a brief silence, then Mistra said, 'I'd like my purse. The one I left behind that first night.'

The fact that she made no attempt to confirm or deny the marriage chilled him. Stephens opened the bottom drawer of his desk; and, without a word, handed her the bag. She emptied the contents onto the desk, and replaced them one by one. She looked up. 'Where are the keys?'

'Oh!' He reached into his pocket, and held them out to her. As she took them, he said, 'I'm coming up to see all of you tonight. You've probably heard.'

She looked at him rather oddly. 'You'll be interested to know that Tannahill has recovered his memory. Accordingly, you haven't a friend left in the group.'

Stephens gazed at her steadily for a moment. 'None?' he

asked.

Her voice was even. 'None.'

Stephens smiled grimly. He was being unloaded all right, all along the line. They didn't realize that it couldn't be done, not while he had breath in his body. He said, 'You can tell Mr. Tannahill that he can't fire me. I'm an employee of Walter Peeley. When Mr. Peeley relieves me of my job, I'll consider myself separated.'

The irony of that held him briefly. If it was Peeley there in the grave, then it might take a little while to dismiss Allison Stephens.

Mistra was speaking. 'Very well, we shall have Mr. Peeley notify you formally.'

'What about us? When you said you loved me – was that just part of your strategy?'

'No,' she said, but her face did not soften. 'But I'll get over it – I've got hundreds of years to recover. And some day – maybe there'll be someone else.'

The coldness of her voice stiffened him. He realized that he had to make a stronger impression than this. He said, 'Is the mind-reader still with you?'

She nodded, questioningly.

'Fire her,' said Stephens. 'She's no good.'

'Are you still harping on the Peeley theme?'

Stephens hesitated. 'Where is Peeley? Has he turned up yet?'

Her reply was slow. 'Not yet,' she said at last. 'But don't worry. We're ready for him. If he's plotting against us—'

'He isn't.' Stephens spoke slowly. 'I missed the boat there – I think.'

'Then who is?'

'I don't know.' He leaned forward earnestly. 'Mistra, you're all in danger of being murdered.'

Mistra shook her head, and smiled ironically. 'Allison, you're being very melodramatic, and also very obvious. You're trying to frighten the group into accepting you. It won't work. I assure you we're not in danger of being exterminated. We've never been more alert.'

She started to pick up her gloves. Stephens said, 'Mistra – wait!'

She settled slowly back in her chair. Her green eyes were questioning. Stephens said, 'Can't you see that I'm trying to help you? I have information.'

'What information?'

Stephens had no intention of sharing with this coldly hostile young woman what the robot-brain of the ship had told him. Besides, his plan of attack now included putting the ultimate pressure on them, if necessary; and for that *he* needed information. He said, 'Mistra, is there any way in which the Grand House could be destroyed?'

She laughed. 'You don't think I'd tell anybody that, do you?'

Stephens leaned forward. '*For your very life*, reconsider that answer.'

Her eyes widened. 'Why, that's ridiculous. Do you suggest that a member of the group could be so stupid? The house is all we've got, actually.'

Stephens said grimly, 'I'm suggesting, on the basis of what I know, that must be the purpose of the traitor. Therefore – have you any quick way of destroying it so that it could never be useful to you again? A new explosive, perhaps. I don't mean anything as large as an atomic bomb, but something a person might carry in his pocket. I admit that's a large order.'

She hesitated, then nodded. 'I can't see any harm in telling you, since you couldn't possibly use the knowledge against us. Element 167 is a physical freak. Released in a fine powder, it would cause atomic instability in the marble of the house that would disintegrate it, so that we could never hope to recover the material in its original form.'

'Element 167? There's nothing else that could do it?'

'That's all, as far as we know.'

'Thanks.' He was silent; finally: 'I'm sorry I can't say, "This is the man!" Maybe you could tell me a little about some of your people. How many are in town right now?'

'Forty-one.'

'Out of fifty-three.' Stephens spoke musingly. 'It would be quite a catch if he got them all.' He went on firmly. 'They've all got to be there. He's got to think that this is his one opportunity. It's the only way to force him into the open. You can see that, can't you?'

Mistra was standing up. She began to put on her gloves. She said, 'I think I can guarantee you a hearing tonight.' She hesitated. 'But if you can't produce, you're a dead man.' Her voice was low and earnest. 'Having brought back Tannahill's memory, and surrendered him, I just have one vote. There's nothing I can do for you, nor will I even try to do it. You're on your own.'

She turned, and left the office. Stephens waited a few minutes, then went out and said to Miss Chainer, 'If anyone comes before you leave, tell them I'll be back about six.'

He went downstairs, waited for an opportune moment, and then made his way down to the sub-basement without being seen. Once in the cave, he felt safe and headed as swiftly as possible for the robot ship. His tension mounted, nevertheless, as he drew near it. Would the robot brain admit him?

His relief as he saw that the door was open almost choked him. But the reality braced him also. He was still considered trustworthy. His plan must be at least partly acceptable.

As he approached the greenish globe, a picture formed on it. He was shown exactly on what trays in the stock rooms he would find element 167, and also what elements would combine with it to nullify its destructive power. The robot seemed to believe that element 221, a gas, would best serve the purpose Stephens had in mind.

Stephens secured a tube each of the two elements, and returned to the globe. But there were no more pictures. The robot-brain evidently could give him no further help. If it were Peeley's body in the Tannahill grave, that was something the machine could not verify for him.

Gloomily, Stephens returned to the Palms Building. Miss Chainer was already gone, but as he entered his private office, he saw that he had a visitor.

Walter Peeley sat in the big chair behind his desk.

19

As they exchanged greetings, Stephens watched the other, baffled. The appearance of Peeley – after logic had consigned him to the role of dead man – did not affect his plan for the showdown that night. But it did place a serious strain on his imagination.

If it wasn't Peeley in the grave . . . then who was it?

Peeley had never, it seemed to Stephens, looked in better health. His face had that vaguely Indian look – so hard to identify in some members of the race – but it was a healthy appearance; there was plenty of color in his cheeks.

Peeley said, 'I've just come from having a talk with Frank Howland. He tells me you and he have a plan for arresting most of the members of the group that's been leeching off the Tannahill estate all these years.'

The shock of the remark held Stephens dumb for several seconds. He was astounded that the district attorney could have been so indiscreet. He said lamely, 'How much did Howland tell you?'

It struck him instantly that the remark might sound critical of Howland having told anything. Stephens went on quickly, 'What I mean is, if I can get an idea of what you already know, I can fill in the gaps.'

Listening, then, he slowly realized that Howland had told everything. By the time Peeley had finished, Stephens' mind was adjusted to the betrayal. It didn't matter. The notion of having the group arrested for carrying weapons without a license, and then stripping off their masks, had never promised to be more than a minor irritation. It might take the pressure off Tannahill. For a time they might be involved with the law. Perhaps, after innumerable delays, prison sentences might actually be dealt out.

But it wouldn't break up the group. It wouldn't identify Peeley's murderous and ambitious colleague. And it wouldn't affect in any way the other aspects of his plan, one of which involved a very unpleasant surprise for Peeley himself.

There was of course the fact that Peeley was one of the two conspirators among the group. Perhaps, under the circumstances, he might not warn the others.

At Peeley's suggestion, the two of them had dinner in town. It was during the meal that it suddenly seemed incredible to Stephens that Howland would have told the plan to Peeley. The district attorney had too much at stake. In ordering Tannahill's arrest, he had made an error dangerous to his career. But then where had Peeley got his information?

Sitting there at the table, a new suspicion came to Stephens.

The man in the grave was Frank Howland. Killing him was part of the precaution that Peeley had taken against his treacherous companion. The robot brain had not been able to show just how Peeley was protecting himself, but now it seemed obvious.

The decisive factor was that Peeley had originally hired Howland, a man of his own build and general physical appearance. While agent of the estate, Howland had become district attorney. Once established in that position, he had been given the opportunity to notice a similarity between an eighteenth century and a twentieth century signature – whereupon the group had probably been impressed by the swiftness with which Peeley fired him from all connection with the estate.

And so, Peeley had appointed to the agency Allison Stephens, a man of his own build and general appearance.

At the critical moment, the two would be murdered – and Peeley, with headquarters conveniently off in Los Angeles, would don the mask of one or the other, and play either or both roles.

The notion seemed so convincing that Stephens abruptly excused himself, entered a phone booth, and called Howland's office. He was informed that 'Mr. Howland has left'.

He dialed the district attorney's home. The woman who answered said, 'Mr. Howland is not expected home this evening until late.'

Stephens hesitated, half-minded to ask if he were talking to Mrs. Howland. And, if so, if she had noticed anything unusual about her husband the past few days. He decided against it, hung up, and returned slowly to the dinner table. Howland being unreachable was not conclusive proof that his theory was correct, but he had to assume that it was.

'I could show him Tannahill's letter, firing me,' he thought tentatively. 'That might convince him that it wouldn't do any good to kill me; he wouldn't be able to make use of the local agency, which is surely what he had in mind.'

He was still considering bringing out the letter, when Peeley said, 'My idea is that we go to your house as soon as we've eaten, and you can give me a picture of the entire local situation.'

Stephens visualized himself alone in a remote suburban home with Walter Peeley, and that was enough. Promptly, he produced Tannahill's letter.

Peeley read it, and handed it back without immediate comment. He seemed very thoughtful on the drive to the bungalow.

After Stephens had served whiskey and soda, Peeley asked to see the letter again. He read it slowly, and finally said, 'How did you get him down on you?'

'I haven't the faintest idea. I'm hoping to get back in his good graces tonight.'

'Then you intend to carry through with your plan?'

'I couldn't stop it now,' lied Stephens. 'Having made the arrangements with Howland, I'm committed.'

The fact that the man before him probably had the mask of Frank Howland's face in his pocket, ready to don it at a moment's notice, wouldn't necessarily change anything.

He spent the next hour talking about the estate. Peeley seemed to listen with interest, a reaction that was hard to evaluate. It might just mean that he was getting information from a man who had been separated from the organization.

At a quarter of nine, the phone rang. The sound of it made Stephens jump. He picked up the receiver with a hand that shook slightly. He said, 'Allison Stephens talking.'

'Mr. Stephens,' said the man's voice at the other end, 'this is the fingerprint bureau at the police department. We've got the fingerprint identification you asked us about.'

'Yes?' Stephens held his voice calm, but his heart gave a leap.

He hung up presently, feeling blank. And then, slowly, he braced himself. There was nothing to do but carry on as he had planned. He would begin by indicting Walter Peeley. Then would come what, for the others, would be an unexpected climax. And then —

He shook his head uneasily. The anti-climax was as vague, and seemed as deadly, as ever.

20

As Stephens parked his car, he saw that Mistra's machine was there. At least it looked like hers. Several other long cars were also drawn up.

He followed Peeley up the steps, noticing how brightly lighted the house was. Their ring was answered by Gico Aine, looking oddly different and distinguished without her jewels. She led them silently into the living room where eleven people – Stephens counted them – were sitting or standing. He recognized Judge Adams, Judge Porter, Carewell and Grant, Tannahill and Mistra. The two other women and the three other men were strangers to him.

It was Tannahill who came forward, a faint, ironic smile on his face. He did not offer his hand. 'You're Stephens?' he said. It was almost as if he wasn't sure.

Stephens nodded curtly, and then turned to face the group. He was anxious to get started. He had purposely timed his arrival ahead of Howland (by forty minutes) so that he could make his initial accusations, and, if possible, gain the group's approval.

He opened his brief case, took out some papers, and then once more looked around him. He wondered which of the women was the mind-reader. Not that he was worried about what thoughts she might detect. He doubted if she could untangle the complexity of plans he had set in motion, some serious, and others little more than red herrings. He hoped that she would notice that he merely wanted to put the group under pressure, and that the main danger was not from him.

He began solemnly by saying, 'My first concern, naturally, was to serve Mr. Tannahill.'

From the corner of his eyes, he saw that the remark brought a grim smile to Tannahill's face. Stephens went on, 'To that end I have prepared a case which, I think you will agree, will effectively convince the public that Mr. Tannahill is not and never has been guilty of the crime with which he was charged.'

He was aware that Mistra, sitting at the far end of the living room, was looking at him as if she wanted to catch his eye. But he kept his gaze on the men who were gathered in a group near the front of the room.

He made his case against Peeley, simply, straightforwardly, forcefully. And every word he spoke brought realization of how strong the evidence he had would sound in an average courtroom. The secret visits to Almirante, the connection with the gang and the payments of huge sums of money from the Tannahill estate to many people without authorization.

What of course would be finally convincing was the fact that, after – at most – a preliminary hearing, Peeley would disappear forever from the scene. And his 'flight' would be regarded as an admission of guilt.

Several times, as he made his points, Stephens glanced at Peeley. The man sat frowning at the floor, and, twice, as Stephens watched, he shifted in his chair.

The case that Stephens made had nothing to do with immortality, spaceships, or atomic war. It was mundane, being primarily concerned with fitting together the surface facts. ('Newton Tannahill was murdered because he discovered that his property was being milked of vast sums of money.') Stephens described such provable facts as the disappearance of the doctor and the undertaker. ('The nephew was buried in the uncle's grave. Why? Because the uncle's body must have been badly damaged when he was murdered.')

The reason for the murder of John Ford was equally simple as Stephens analyzed it with his deliberately superficial logic. ('He was an incident. He was killed to put pressure on Arthur Tannahill, to force him to sign a letter authorizing continuation of the money payments from the estate.')

Jenkins? ('He saw Peeley that first night, and was murdered to prevent his ever telling anybody that Peeley had been in town.')

Stephens finished his charge by saying: 'It was not my intention to explain the motives which prompted Mr. Peeley to pay out so much wealth that did not belong to him to the parties involved. But I think now that I am justified in pointing out that we must not underestimate the psychological meaning of the Mayan or Aztec cult – I never did distinguish between the two in my own mind – to which he belongs. We have here what might be called cult loyalty ... Ladies and gentlemen, that concludes my case against Walter Peeley.'

He looked directly at Mistra for the first time. Her eyes met his coolly, but she seemed puzzled, also. Stephens smiled tautly, walked to a chair near the hall door, and sat down.

21

The room was almost unchanged. No one besides himself had moved, except for some tiny changes in posture. The two editors were writing in their notebooks. Tannahill sat on a couch, leaning forward; his face was buried in his hands, and he seemed to be laughing. Judge Porter, his smooth face bland, his tinted glasses a shield for any expression that might be in his eyes, stared sardonically at Peeley.

'Well, Mr. Peeley,' he said, 'what have you got to say for yourself?'

At first Peeley said nothing. He sat in a deep chair, and his face was a study. He seemed indecisive. He glanced at Stephens, then as quickly glanced away again. Then he looked at the door that led to the hall. At last he sighed, and stared at Stephens.

'So that's what you've been rushing around about,' he said.

He fell silent again. He seemed to realize that everybody was watching him now, for he laughed harshly, and took a cigarette out of his pocket, placed it nervously in his mouth.

'I'd like to have your explanation again,' he said, 'for my motive in committing these murders. I want to get it straight.'

He listened, his head slightly cocked, as if he were trying to hear some subtler tone than was apparent in the surface of the words that Stephens spoke. When Stephens again described the letter that Tannahill had been asked to sign, the lawyer laughed once more, a harder, more determined laugh. He looked like a man who was stiffening to the tremendousness of his danger.

'You damned fool!' he said. 'You said yourself that I have a letter from Tannahill authorizing me to continue, do you understand? – *to continue* – the payments to these people. It is clear from that letter that Tannahill knew the reason for the payments being made, which is more than I do.'

'You have this letter,' said Stephens gently, 'on you?'

His tone had an effect. Until that instant, Peeley must have thought that this was a move to undermine the strength of the letter. Now, a startled look flashed into his face. His eyes widened. 'Why, you scoundrel,' he said. 'You've been to the office in Los Angeles.'

'I'm sure,' said Stephens quietly, 'you realize that no melodramatic attempt to put over the idea that such a letter ever existed will be particularly convincing to those present.'

Peeley sat down. Amazingly, he seemed to have full control of himself. He looked at Stephens calmly.

Then his gaze turned toward the others. Judge Porter wiped his eyes, and frowned at Peeley. 'You're taking this very hard,' the Judge said. 'I can see you're envisaging the possibility that it might be wise if you did bear the brunt of this. After all, we can't have the owner of the house under a cloud. Also, it would effectively dispose of a very curious fear we've had in connection with you the past few days.' He glanced at the two newspaper publishers. 'What do you think, gentlemen?'

Carewell, a long, gaunt man, who had been whispering to Grant, climbed to his feet. 'My morning extra,' he said, 'will contain a complete exoneration of Mr. Tannahill. The Tannahill family,' he intoned, 'has for generations been the backbone of Almirante. This newspaper, which also has a long and honorable tradition in the city, will not lightly drag down a family so thoroughly American and Californian. In a world beset by uncertainties, almost destroyed by immoral upstarts and creatures without principle, we must turn more and more to people who have roots in the soil of their land, and not to nameless drifters.'

He paused. 'So much,' he said, 'for the murder charge.' He looked at Mistra. 'This is all very ordinary. Your young man is showing good average sense but very little imagination.'

Mistra stood up, and beckoned Stephens. He came over, and let himself be led into a corner. She said in a low tone: 'Is this the great revelation? I thought you told me Peeley was not the man.'

Stephens said angrily: 'Where's that damned mind-reader? Can you bring her over? I want to talk to her.'

Mistra looked at him for a long moment. Without another word, she hurried out of the room. She came back accompanied by a sharp-eyed, pleasant-looking girl. At least, she seemed like a girl till she came up, and Stephens saw that her eyes, despite their sparkle of youth, were calm and wise.

Mistra said, 'This is Triselle.'

Triselle grasped Stephens' hand. Her expression was thoughtful. 'I won't anticipate your next climax.'

'You know about it?'

'It was apparent the moment he walked in. He wouldn't have gotten away with it.'

Stephens said anxiously, 'What else do you know?'

'I haven't found your man. Your informant' – she hesitated – 'I don't know what I mean by that, because I get a picture of darkness. Anyway, whoever told you must be mistaken. There is no one.'

Stephens said curtly, 'Let's not start an argument now. You can or you cannot sense a danger threat.'

'I cannot, except —' She paused.

'Yes?'

'Vaguely.'

'From whom?'

'I – don't know!' She bit her lip as if in vexation. 'I'm sorry I can't even give you a lead.'

Stephens glanced helplessly at Mistra, who shook her head. 'I have only a faint idea what you two are talking about. But then, I generally have that feeling when Triselle is conversing with someone.'

Stephens was silent. Triselle was turning out to be a better mind-reader than he had anticipated. Whoever was fooling her had evidently over the years acquired an enormous skill at concealing his thoughts. He faced the woman again. But she was already shaking her head.

'They all attempted it,' she said. 'They spent hours talking to me, trying first one method of concealment, then another. Occasionally I had the feeling that they were succeeding, but obviously, I couldn't be sure.'

Stephens nodded. 'Their very success would bar you from knowing if the thought had ever occurred at all.' He broke off: 'Who, particularly, gave you the feeling that they were concealing —'

The woman sighed. 'I see you didn't understand me. All of them succeeded at one time or another. I realize now that even you got away with a vital piece of information that night we visited you.'

At the far end of the room, Peeley was climbing to his feet. 'Well, gentlemen, as I see it, it is necessary for me to disappear and bear the brunt of the search for the murderer. I accept the role.'

Stephens walked rapidly into the center of the room. 'Sit down, Mr. Peeley,' he said politely. 'I have a few more remarks to make about you.'

He didn't wait for a reply, but turning to the group, described briefly his analysis of why Frank Howland and Allison Stephens had successively been chosen to be local representative of the estate. Stephens finished: 'I'm going to make the prediction that, in walking out of here in order to "disappear", Mr. Peeley would shortly have walked back in as Mr. Howland.'

He paused to look around; and saw that once again he had an impatient audience. It was amazing, but they still didn't suspect the truth.

Tannahill was staring sardonically at Peeley. 'Up to your old tricks, eh?'

Judge Porter said, 'Walter, you really are incorrigible. But then, I've had ideas like that myself. I never could figure out, though, just how to work them.'

Stephens said, 'Mr. Howland and I worked out a little plan whereby everyone in this room would be arrested for carrying concealed weapons, and have their masks removed. That way they wouldn't even be identified as prominent citizens, and so would be eliminated for a year or more, depending on the sentence meted out.'

Judge Porter shook his head. 'Doesn't sound like a very comprehensive plan. I'm surprised at you, Walter.'

Stephens felt briefly baffled. They were too amoral, this group that had lived so long. Confronted by betrayal, their attitude seemed to be that it was to be expected that certain members would try to seize control of the Grand House.

'Unfortunately,' he said at last, 'another and more deadly disaster befell Mr. Peeley's plan. Picture the scene: He killed John Ford, and wrote the note to Howland. Somewhere along the line he was seen by Jenkins, and had to shoot fast. Or at least he thought he did. He used a needle beam, which I assume he wouldn't have done except in an emergency. And then, with all that preparation behind him, he made a fateful error.'

Stephens had come to the climax of his attack aware that Peeley was beginning to fidget. He was aware of it out of the corner of one eye, because the man was standing slightly behind and to one side of him.

Peeley said: 'I'm going to get out of here. This is too melodramatic for me.'

'Before you go,' said Stephens, *take off that mask!*'

As he spoke, he snatched his Nambu, and pointed it. His move did not seem to disturb the others, for no weapons came out. But his words had a profound effect. Several men jumped to their feet. Tannahill, who had been standing, said sharply: 'Mask!'

Stephens waited till there was silence again, then gently: 'Take it off, my friend. You acted in self-defense. You have my personal assurance that you're going to get away with it whether the group likes it or not.' He broke off. 'Somebody help him with that thing. There must be a quick way of getting it off.'

Triselle came forward. She had a bottle of colorless liquid. 'Hold out your hands!' she said.

Peeley hesitated, then shrugged, and let her pour about half the chemical into his cupped palms. His hands went up, then came down.

Frank Howland stood before them.

His face twisted into a scowl. His teeth showed as he said: 'All right, so I'll have to be careful about what I do against you. I killed Peeley in self-defense, but I can't afford a murder charge.'

Stephens frowned. The words did not show a sharp enough understanding of the situation. 'Howland,' he said, 'what do you know about the activities of' – he waved vaguely at the room – 'these people?'

Howland looked surprised. 'But you told me that. A cult ... Once I got involved' – he broke off curtly. 'Never mind.'

Stephens glanced around at the other people. Tannahill was staring stonily at the floor. Judge Porter watched Howland with what seemed a speculative expression. Mistra and the mind-reader were talking together in low tones. Grimly, he realized that they shared his view. This man was not a threat.

And still he was not satisfied. 'Howland,' he said, 'where did you get the mask of Peeley's face?'

There was a stir. All over the room people looked up.

Howland hesitated. 'It came in the mail,' he said. There was perspiration on his forehead. 'The note along with it told me how to use it, reminded me of my acting career – that is, my ability to imitate voices – and suggested I use it. Or else the writer would tell the police where Peeley's body was buried.'

'What was supposed to be your reason for all this – if you were caught?'

'I was to say that I was after money. Frankly...' Howland shrugged. 'I couldn't bring myself to that. But if pressed I was to tell the truth.'

'After tonight, you're in the clear – is that right?'

'Yes.'

Stephens studied the man. He was disappointed. He did not doubt what Howland was saying. But it seemed hard to believe that Howland had actually been trapped into such a situation. Was it possible he had merely been tricked into believing that he had committed murder? If so, the final explanation would have to wait.

He walked with Howland to the outside door. He said, 'I'll come in to see you tomorrow. We can talk this over.'

Howland nodded. There were lines of strain in his face. 'Christ,' he said, 'I'm glad to get out of that room. What's the matter with those people?'

It was a question Stephens did not attempt to answer. His mind was already on the greater danger. In a tense voice he asked, 'Where have you got the police spotted?'

Howland said, 'You don't think I was fool enough to bring the police in on this?'

'What!'

With an effort Stephens controlled his dismay. He had a flashing mind-picture of the time it would take to organize a police force large enough to patrol the grounds. And he realized it would be too slow.

He watched Howland go down the steps, and swiftly he walked across the terrace, and stepped down into the first patio area. He whistled softly. And waited.

A figure moved out of the shadows. The shadowy shape whispered, 'Riggs!' Then it shoved a slip of paper into Stephens' hand, and retreated into the darkness.

Stephens hurried back toward the front door. As he came opposite a window, he hastily read the note that the detective had given him. It read:

All set.

Stephens crumpled the note, put it in his pocket, and walked back into the living room.

Outside, the small man adjusted his mask of Riggs' face. And moved slowly towards one of the patio doors.

Several people had joined the group during his absence. They sat or stood now in that oak-paneled room with its line of French doors running the length of the spacious patio. All the doors but one were closed.

Stephens counted twelve men and six women in the room, other than himself. And they were all looking at him.

Ignoring them, he walked rapidly over to the mind-reader. She shook her head, and said, 'The menace seemed to grow a while ago, but it's faded again. I can see more clearly now what you're afraid of. I don't sense anything like that.'

Stephens glanced at Mistra. 'How many people are there in the House?'

'Forty.'

'Who's missing?' Tensely. 'Didn't you say there were forty-one in town?'

'I included Peeley,' she said simply.

Stephens started to turn away. Then he faced her again. 'They're all here *this* minute?'

It was Triselle who answered that. 'No, Tezla went out to search the yards twenty minutes ago.'

The question and the answer had been loud enough for everyone in the room to hear. Now, there was silence. Briefly, Stephens was drawn from his own inner tension. Here were eighteen immortals. He studied them curiously. In spite of their expensive clothing, the men were a motley lot. Fate had taken no trouble to select impressive types. Without exception, however, the women were good looking. It seemed to suggest why they had been chosen.

Possibly, each person was going over in his or her mind

the associations each had had with the grim little Indian. Stephens waited till they began to stir, then said, 'I saw a picture. It included Peeley and a man about Tezla's size, but it didn't look like him.'

He broke off savagely: 'Damn those perfect masks of yours! They make it possible for anyone to be anyone. I saw Tezla twice. Did I see him as he is, or was that a mask?'

'A mask!' It was Tannahill.

Stephens swore aloud. 'Is he an Indian?'

'Yes.'

There was a pause. 'This picture you saw,' said Tannahill. 'When was it taken?'

'About two thousand years ago,' Stephens replied.

Tannahill twisted about, and said in a clipped tone of command: 'Search the grounds! Guard every door! Bring him in here if he's around. We'll settle this thing right now.'

'*Wait!*'

Stephens' voice cut sharply across the room, and stopped in mid-stride men who were heading toward the doors. Tannahill turned, and faced him; and now the difference between the man who had lost his memory and the man who had recovered it was noticeable. It showed in the lips and in the eyes. The eyes of Tanequila the Bold peered forth through tensed eyelids. His lips were compressed into a thin line.

He said, 'Stephens, what the hell do you mean, giving orders?'

Stephens said, 'The moment any of those doors open — that will be the signal for an agent of mine to toss element 167 onto one of the marble patios or onto the terrace, or even into the house itself!'

Stephens went on quickly, 'There is no reason for alarm — if we have properly identified our man. Now, I'm going to suggest how he should be handled —'

'We'll handle him in our own way,' said Tannahill in an arrogant tone, 'according to our constitution.'

'You'll handle him,' said Stephens, 'as I suggest — and, my

friend, I might as well inform you that your reign of absolute power is over. I have in my brief case more than fifty copies of an authorization – which you will sign – converting this house into a Foundation, and we will as a group form the board of directors. I've named you first chairman, but I've included my own name on the board.'

He went on grimly, 'You'd better start signing, because I won't call my agent inside here till there's a copy available for every member of the group. Somebody get out those documents!'

It was Mistra who secured them. Her eyes glinted as she brought them to a table near Tannahill, who glanced at them angrily, and seemed about to speak. Stephens cut him off:

'Quick, man! Ask your mind-reader if I'm not telling the truth. I *have* got element 167. There *is* an agent outside ready to do exactly as I've said.'

'Triselle!' It was Mistra. 'Is that true?'

'Yes.'

Tannahill snarled, 'But why didn't you warn us? What the hell do you mean —'

'Because he means well,' said the woman quietly. 'And you don't think I was going to interfere with him while he was searching so desperately for the person among us who —'

Stephens interrupted, 'We've got to let Tezla off easily. Think of all the years he's been carrying the burden of a conviction that, as the survivor of the first group in the house, he was its rightful owner. Now, he's out in the open. The tension is bound to fade.'

He broke off. 'Tannahill – start signing. Don't forget, we've still got to catch him. We've still got to persuade him.'

The owner of the Grand House hesitated a moment longer. Then abruptly drew out a pen, and began to scrawl his signature.

Stephens handed the copies first to the men. When ten had been signed, when he had one in his own breast pocket, he went to the door and called Riggs. As the little detective entered, men began to stream out into the grounds.

'Well, sir,' said Riggs, 'I see we're getting action. What's the latest?'

Stephens said, 'Let me have that capsule you've got.'

Riggs handed it over promptly, and Stephens walked over and gave it to Mistra. 'Tezla will have some of this element from your secret laboratories, of course,' he said. 'As I analyze his plan, his sole purpose in having me go aboard the ship—'

'Ship?' said Mistra.

Stephens ignored her. Now, that the documents were being signed, he intended to tell them about the ship that had come from the stars twenty centuries before. But that was for later. At the moment, he went on:

'— purpose in having me go aboard the ship was to find out if the robot brain was still in operation.'

'Robot brain? Allison, what are you talking about?'

'If it were,' said Stephens, 'then all he had to do was destroy the house, whereupon the robot brain would have to deal with him. There wouldn't be any further use for it to hope—'

He grew aware that Triselle had come up beside them. The telepath said, 'That little man who just went out into the hall – who is he?'

Stephens half-turned. 'Don't worry about Riggs,' he said. 'If anyone is all right, it's—'

He stopped. He had a curious, sinking sensation. He had had the impression that Tannahill had contacted the detective haphazardly out of a Los Angeles telephone book.

But Tannahill had not actually said that. Stephens remembered the scene with sudden clarity. He said in a choked voice, 'What do you get from his mind?'

The mind-reader said, 'Placid thoughts. He's a little worried. If he's disguising a determination to destroy the house, it's a wonderful job.'

Stephens went over to Tannahill, who said, 'I don't remember the period very well. I recall we were in the bar together, and he bought me a drink —'

'But did you phone him first?'

'Phone him – no, of course not.'

Stephens glanced at the door that led to the hall. Riggs was not in sight. 'He'll go down into the museum,' Stephens thought in agony, 'release his own element 167 and go down into the tunnel to force the robot —'

He hurried to the hall door, slowed as he reached it, and walked casually out into the gleaming hall. Riggs was nowhere in sight.

Stephens ran all the way to the steps, and started down them. He was moving cautiously now, careful not to make any sounds.

The glass door at the bottom was open. Through it, Stephens could see Riggs lifting the lid of one of the display cases.

Stephens snatched from his own pocket the small tube he had taken from the robot ship. With his finger firmly hooked into the release key, he stepped across the threshold.

'Oh, Riggs!' he said.

The man turned with a terrible casualness. 'I was just admiring this Toltec art object,' he said. 'Very interesting.'

It was an odd time to be appreciating art. Stephens said, 'Riggs – Tezla – you can still save your life. You can't win now. Give up!'

There was a long silence. The little man turned and looked directly at him. 'Stephens,' he croaked, 'You and I can rule the world!'

'Not without the Grand House. Close off that element!'

'We don't need the house – don't you see? We've got the robot ship. We can get from it all the information we need. Once the others are out of the way, it'll have to —'

A vague, bluish glow was coming from the display case. Stephens said in a piercing tone: 'Shut it off! Quick!'

'It would cost me my hand now. Stephens, listen!'

'It's your hand or your life! Hurry! I've got element 221 right here. There's nothing in all the world like it. Chemically, it will unite with your 167 to —'

His finger squeezed the release even as he tossed the tube straight at Riggs. The needle beam from the weapon in Riggs' hand missed him, because he ducked, turned and raced up the steps.

The room behind him shuddered. A bluish haze of smoke billowed up the steps.

Then darkness.

'... Do you, Mistra Lanett, take this man to be your lawfully wedded husband?'

'I do.' Her voice was steady...

Afterward, in her car, she said to Stephens, 'I felt odd. Do you realize that this is the *first* time I've ever been married?'

Stephens said nothing. He was thinking of the robot-ship buried under the Grand House. Soon, it would be resuming its long-delayed journey. And there was an idea in his mind; it made him breathless to think of it: *Why shouldn't Mistra and he go along?*

'Personally,' Mistra said, almost irrelevantly, 'I want a girl. Boys are all right but —'

Stephens sighed. These women with their home and children notions. Here was the vastest imaginable world of adventure beckoning, and she was intent on procreation. He turned to look at her and his dream of adventure was lost in the softness of her gaze. There were more worlds in the greenness of her eyes than he could possibly imagine in the universe.

'A girl *and* a boy,' he said as his lips found hers. Their eagerness denied their immortality and he was aware that forever could wait.

THE WORLD'S GREATEST SCIENCE FICTION AUTHORS NOW AVAILABLE IN PANTHER BOOKS

E E 'Doc' Smith

'Classic Lensman Series'

Masters of the Vortex	85p	☐
Children of the Lens	85p	☐
Second Stage Lensman	85p	☐
Grey Lensman	85p	☐
Galactic Patrol	75p	☐
First Lensman	85p	☐
Triplanetary	85p	☐
'Lensman' Gift Set	£4.25	☐

'Skylark Series'

The Skylark of Space	75p	
Skylark Three	75p	☐
The Skylark of Valeron	85p	☐
Skylark Duquesne	85p	☐
'Skylark' Gift Set	£3.25	☐

'Family D'Alembert Series' (with Stephen Goldin)

The Imperial Stars	75p	☐
Stranglers' Moon	75p	☐
The Clockwork Traitor	75p	☐
Getaway World	85p	☐
The Bloodstar Conspiracy	65p	☐
The Purity Plot	75p	☐

'Novels'

Subspace Explorers	85p	☐
Galaxy Primes	50p	☐
Spacehounds of IPC	85p	☐

THE WORLD'S GREATEST SCIENCE FICTION AUTHORS NOW AVAILABLE IN PANTHER BOOKS

Poul Anderson

Fire Time	75p ☐
Orbit Unlimited	60p ☐
Long Way Home	50p ☐
The Corridors of Time	50p ☐
Time and Stars	50p ☐
After Doomsday	50p ☐
Star Fox	40p ☐
Trader to the Stars	35p ☐

Philip José Farmer

The Stone God Awakens	80p ☐
Time's Last Gift	50p ☐
Traitor to the Living	85p ☐
To Your Scattered Bodies Go	85p ☐
The Fabulous Riverboat	85p ☐
Strange Relations	35p ☐
The Dark Design	£1.25 ☐

All these books are available at your local bookshop or newsagent, or can be ordered direct from the publisher. Just tick the titles you want and fill in the form below.

Name ....

Address ....

....

Write to Panther Cash Sales, PO Box 11, Falmouth, Cornwall TR10 9EN.

Please enclose remittance to the value of the cover price plus:

UK: 25p for the first book plus 10p per copy for each additional book ordered to a maximum charge of £1.05.

BFPO and EIRE: 25p for the first book plus 10p per copy for the next 8 books, thereafter 5p per book.

OVERSEAS: 40p for the first book and 12p for each additional book.

Granada Publishing reserve the right to show new retail prices on covers, which may differ from those previously advertised in the text or elsewhere.